ATTACK
OF THE
BLACK
RECTANGLES

ATTACK
OF THE
BLACK
RECTANGLES

Amy Sarig King

SCHOLASTIC PRESS
NEW YORK

Library of Congress Cataloging-in-Publication Data available

ISBN 978-1-338-68052-2

10 9 8 7 6 5 4 3 2 1   22 23 24 25 26

Printed in the U.S.A.   37

First edition, September 2022

Book design by Abby Dening and Elizabeth B. Parisi

For the truth tellers

IF YOU CAN'T BE DIRECT, WHY BE?

—*Lily Tomlin*

. . . TO BE AFRAID OF WHAT IS DIFFERENT
OR UNFAMILIAR IS TO BE AFRAID OF LIFE.

—*Theodore Roosevelt*

A STRONG SPIRIT TRANSCENDS RULES.

—*Prince*

The Adults Around Here

PROLOGUE

"I am here to protect all of us from the ugly world."
—Laura Samuel Sett

A ccording to a lot of the adults in our town, everything here is perfect.

We don't have accidents. We don't have any crime at all. We don't have Halloween anymore. Or junk food. We don't have bad thoughts. We don't use any bad words, like ~~cancer~~ or ~~death~~ or ~~sex~~ or ~~donut~~.

A lot of people thank Ms. Laura Samuel Sett for this. She's as famous as a person can get in our town, and probably the only reason the local newspaper is still in print. Everyone reads her letters there.

Ms. Sett is also a sixth-grade teacher, but the adults around here are her students as much as kids like me who pass through her classroom at Independence North Elementary School. Those adults join Ms. Sett in letter writing, sitting on the town council and committees, and making rule after rule after rule. They seem to believe that rules equal safety—by making more rules, they are keeping us all safe and keeping the town's reputation spotless.

Ms. Sett thinks that if we even think about "bad things," our whole town could fall right into the toilet of the world.

"Just like all those other towns," she says.

The adults around here don't just keep our town safe from unsavory words and thoughts. They keep our town safe from unsavory people, too. And if we believe what the adults around here say, then unsavory people are anyone who doesn't go to church, anyone who doesn't pledge the flag louder than the person next to them, and anyone who eats junk food.

Most of us have to go to the next town over to do our grocery shopping so we can buy Cheetos.

■

My family has ignored the town's silly rules for as long as I can remember. We don't go to church, I don't pledge the flag overly loudly, and we eat a decent amount of junk food. My mom loves Oreos. I love Cheetos. And my grandad is a bona fide candy freak.

Ms. Sett wrote a letter to the paper one time about an elderly man who sits on Main Street, always eating candy. She asked for him to be removed for his bad example to children. She was talking about Grandad. Here's what he did in response: He started bringing me with him.

Don't get me wrong—we eat really good homemade food and a lot of fruits and vegetables, and I get a lot of calcium and vitamins and grains and protein and all the other stuff in the food pyramid.

There are much worse things in the world than junk food. Mom knows it because she works at a place that helps people grieve the death of their loved ones and helps people with cancer and other terminal illnesses. Grandad knows it because he fought in the Vietnam War. My dad sure knows it, because he's always mad at something—like, every single day.

I just think Ms. Sett and the adults around here should mind their own business. I don't think any town is perfect and I don't think any town is in the toilet of the world. I think life is what life is and we just have to try our best.

Life is what life is and we just have to try our best. —Mac Delaney

For all I'm about to say here about her and for all her weird rules, Ms. Sett taught me to stand up for myself and I'm grateful to her for that.

You're probably confused.

Yes, Ms. Sett is a pain and thinks we shouldn't eat Cheetos. But also yes, she was nice to me when I needed it most.

No one is ever just one thing.

And not everyone is telling the truth.

That's the closest anyone will ever get to perfect.

Last Year—BOT DUCK MAN

W e were on the way to Philadelphia with the fifth-grade school trip when Denis and I made up the game BOT DUCK MAN. It stands for *botfly*, *duck*, and *human*.

Botfly on account of Denis's uncle getting one in his arm the last time he went to Costa Rica. *Duck* because we live in a town with a lot of ducks, and ducks eat insects including, we figured, botflies. *Human* on account of the way Denis described the botfly coming out of his uncle's arm—right by the elbow—and how bad his uncle said it hurt.

I am never going to Costa Rica.

Anyway, it's just like ROCK PAPER SCISSORS and I highly recommend it as an alternative to listening to the tour guide at the Liberty Bell.

"Stop it."

Those were the first two words I ever heard from Ms. Sett. She was a chaperone because the school always had sixth-grade teachers chaperone fifth-grade trips.

"Stop it," she said again, and then she moved Denis to the other side of the Liberty Bell so we couldn't finish our BOT DUCK MAN tournament. I was winning.

BOT beats MAN.

DUCK beats BOT.

MAN beats DUCK.

After the Liberty Bell, we went to Independence Hall, where the tour guide was way more boring than the Liberty Bell tour guide.

And no, I don't have a bad attitude. I've seen the Liberty Bell and Independence Hall three other times and each time I wasn't impressed. It's not that I don't respect the founding fathers, but I do have some problems with how they did stuff. Mostly how they bought and sold people. I definitely have a problem with that.

So when it was question time at the end of the tour, and we were standing right in the room where the founding fathers had signed the Declaration of Independence, I raised my hand and asked, "How many of the guys who signed the Declaration of Independence owned slaves?"

Ms. Sett moved quickly toward me with her hand out.

The tour guide said, "Forty-one out of fifty-six signers owned slaves. That's a great question."

"Thanks," I said.

I'm white, so maybe this seems like a weird question. But just because I'm white doesn't mean I can't talk about what white people do wrong. We do a lot wrong. For starters, we don't talk about how 73 percent of the signers of the Declaration of Independence owned slaves.

Ms. Sett stopped edging toward me once the tour guide answered. But she gave me a disapproving look while she listened to the next question. Marci Thompson asked something about why women weren't invited to the whole signing party. Predictable. Marci was always talking about women and how they need more rights. I'd been stuck in the same class as her since first grade. The whole time, I thought she was okay . . . as long as you didn't say anything to her.

Ms. Sett didn't say anything to Marci then. Or me.

But I could tell she was taking notes in her head.

On the bus home from the Philadelphia trip, the teachers made us sing "Row, Row, Row Your Boat" like we were first graders. They made us do it in three different groups of singers so we could appreciate "the harmonies!" Denis and I were playing a best-out-of-twenty-one tournament of BOT DUCK MAN. He won both games during "Row, Row, Row Your Boat" because I can't sing and think at the same time. Then I lost my place in the song and sang out of sync with everyone until I just stopped singing altogether.

Marci Thompson leaned around the seat in front of us and chided, "You two should really pay more attention."

"Are you a teacher now?" Denis asked.

"Trying to be a good friend," she said.

Denis looked like he was going to say something mean. So I said, "You're a great friend, Marci, but you could probably be more chilled out."

My mom taught me how to do that.

What Grace Is

My mom knows a lot about grace. As I said, she works in hospice care, which is technically where people who know they're going to die go so they can die in peace. Once people die, she then helps their loved ones through their grief, and if that isn't the most graceful thing I've ever heard of, I don't know what is.

Another reason Mom needs grace is her dad, my grandad. He lives in our basement in what he calls the "old fogey flat." He says *flat* instead of *apartment* because he married Gram, who was from a place called Cornwall in England. He's American, 100 percent, but he adopted words from her like *flat* instead of *apartment*, *bin* instead of *trash can*, and a lot of other ones I can't remember unless he's using them.

Grandad has his own kind of grace. It's loud. Loud grace looks like attending protests and writing letters to the president about veterans' benefits and civil rights. Sometimes he stands on the front porch and yells at anyone driving by our house at more than twenty-five miles per hour to "SLOW DOWN!"

An even bigger reason Mom needs grace is my dad. He hasn't lived with us since I was eight, but he still comes around to work on Grandad's old car with me on Saturdays. This was how he and Mom arranged it when he moved into a place where he can't have me stay on weekends. He eats dinner with us on Saturday, too, which can get tricky sometimes because he's hard to deal with, but Mom's grace is unconditional—with mashed potatoes and gravy.

Dad likes to tell me he isn't from Earth, originally. He isn't even from our galaxy. And the car he's working on in the garage isn't really a car—it's a spacecraft.

That's our secret. It's also one reason he can be so hard to deal with. It's difficult to get someone to follow Earth rules when they think they don't apply.

He first told me about it a long time ago, when I was too young to worry about why he was being so weird. He says he's some kind of alien anthropologist—a sort of scientist who studies other cultures.

One time when I was seven, he yelled at all of us for not telling him that the neighbors got a rabbit hutch. Mom said to me after Dad stormed out to take a walk, "He's just upset he didn't know before us, that's all."

I went to my room and tried to figure out the real reason why he was so mad. About rabbits. I considered that on his planet, rabbits might be venomous. I couldn't wait to ask him about it. But when he got home that night, he pretended that it never happened, so the rest of us pretended, too.

Being around people who pretend something didn't happen when it did happen requires grace. Accepting that Dad doesn't live with us anymore requires grace. Helping him work on Grandad's car every Saturday while he barely talks to me requires grace. Acting like this is all normal requires grace.

Grace is a good thing to have.

It's like jam. It sweetens things.

Summer

Our school doesn't tell us who our teacher is until the week before school starts. It's one of the old rules that people follow even though it doesn't make any sense. Denis hates it because he has anxiety and he really should know who his teacher is so he can mentally prepare for it.

My job during the summer is to keep Denis so busy he doesn't think about what teacher he might get. We play a lot of BOT DUCK MAN.

June is a good month to walk around town and go to the big park and feed the ducks. It isn't too hot and the tourists are in full bloom. They usually stop here to eat and shop between Amish farm and buggy outings and tours of the pretzel house on Main Street—America's first pretzel bakery. We are also home to the longest-running Fourth of July celebration and the oldest American boarding school for girls, founded in 1746. We have horse parking all over town, so I guess that's "charming," as Mom would say. Actual signs read: HORSE PARKING ONLY.

If I was a tourist, I'd come here just for those signs.

July is mostly video games in the air-conditioning and playing in the creek at the small park. For Fourth of July, my whole family stays overnight at a cabin way out in the Pennsylvania forest reserve so Grandad doesn't have to hear fireworks. This year we decide to stay for five whole days.

In August, Denis goes to summer camp for two weeks and I play *Ultimate Detective*, my favorite mystery video game, for twelve days in a row. Grandad sits and watches me play, so it's not like I'm by myself in a dark room. Plus, Grandad and I are walkers—Sunday walks, morning walks, holiday walks, and in summer, a lot of night walks.

Once Denis comes home from camp with all his cool walking sticks and stories about campfires and hikes, it's time to find out what teacher we got.

Denis asks me on the phone, "Are you scared?"

I answer, "No."

I never mind what teacher I get, so long as I can read

books when I want to, keep my desk messy because I like it that way, and pick projects and write reports on things that interest me.

My motto is: If it's not interesting, I don't care.

No teacher I've ever met has been okay with my motto, but I keep hoping.

Denis and I both get Ms. Sett for sixth grade. So does Marci Thompson.

The thing I say to Denis on the phone that day, while he's panicking because Ms. Sett has a reputation for caring about posture and Denis is a chronic sloucher, is "Whatever happens this year, you're going to be fine."

"She's going to bug me every day about that piece of my hair that sticks up in the back," Denis stresses.

"Cowlicks are not illegal."

"Neither is slouching . . . and I heard she makes kids sit with a board behind their back," he says.

"She probably doesn't," I assure him. "Let's go run around. You'll feel better if you get some energy out."

"I can't even get out of bed," Denis says.

"You went back to bed?"

"Yes."

"Because of this?"

"Yes."

"What if you'd gotten either of the other two teachers?" I ask.

"I would still be in bed," Denis answers. So I walk to his house and we play BOT DUCK MAN on his bed for two hours.

That night I dream of a plywood torture device, and Denis is strapped inside. He sits so straight, his spine is fusing in a perfect ninety-degree angle to his legs. I have to save him.

In the dream, the only things that can save him are Cheetos and soda.

Table Assignments

Usually, on the first day of school, we get assigned to tables. Tables are five or six desks all smashed together with name tags stuck to the tops. That's how it's been since kindergarten.

But in Ms. Sett's room, all the desks are lined up like soldiers, all facing front, and there aren't any plants. That's always a bad sign. No plants. Plus, it's super hot because the day is way too warm for September and the school's air-conditioning is broken.

Ms. Sett stands outside the door smiling and saying, "Welcome all! Welcome! How do you do?" like she's from the twentieth century or something.

"Just find your desk and sit, and you may place those on my desk before you sit down," she says. Denis has a three-pack of tissues, Marci has two big bottles of hand sanitizer. I came empty-handed. We're all sweating a little bit—but the girls look really uncomfortable because they're not allowed to wear shorts.

When everyone finds their seats, Ms. Sett moves to the front of the room. She's wearing a dress with green triangles on it—different shades of green and different-sized triangles—and she wears a triangle bracelet that matches. Her hair is a little shorter than Mom's, right to her shoulder, and she looks about thirty-five years old, if I was to guess, even though her letters in the paper read like she's from a black-and-white movie.

She's sweating, too, but seems to be fine with it, even as it drips down the side of her face.

She says, "I am so excited about this school year for all of you! Sixth grade! Your last here at Independence Elementary. So much to learn!" She claps her hands together excitedly.

"There are some things you need to know about this classroom, though, folks. It's all about rules. We don't tolerate any of the behaviors your age group usually indulges in, so you can forget about giggling, goofing off, or making funny noises with your armpits. If you take out your phone for any reason whatsoever, I will drop it in the tank of water at the back of the class, and you'll get its useless skeleton back at the end of the day. Forget also about talking to each other, passing notes, and bad posture. Never forget posture, students! Sit up straight and smile!"

Denis winces.

"In this classroom, you will be treated like an adult. And if you behave in the way I'm asking you to behave, there will be numerous benefits. The first being very little homework."

A joyful murmur moves through the classroom. It makes her smile.

"The way I want you to see this year of your education is like college. *You* get to choose what you want to learn about, *you* get to choose the books you read off our class list, and *you* get to make your own study schedules. If you do poorly, it's on you. If you do well, your grades will reflect it. Sound good?"

I look around. Everyone is nodding. As I nod with them, I can feel my mouth hanging open. I'm starstruck. This is the kind of teacher I've wanted my whole if-it's-not-interesting-I-don't-care life.

At lunch, Denis complains about how she split us up— me by the window, him over by the door. Marci says,

"And me right in the middle!" But all I can do is dream of sixth-grade college. I'm already writing reports in my head about botflies so I don't have to learn about boring things like names for types of clouds. And I'm sick of learning half-truths instead of history, so maybe I can do a project on something completely true for once—like why it's not a cool touristy thing that the pretzel house on Main Street highlights the musket slats in the building and the fact that they could shoot at Native Americans through them. Maybe I can write about how it wasn't okay to be shooting at the rightful caretakers of the land. For the record, that would be the Susquehannock and Lenni Lenape tribes.

"Are you even listening to us?" Denis asks.

"Sorry," I tell them. "She's just not what I expected."

Marci says, "She certainly acts a lot cooler than people told me."

"I read her letters in the paper and she seems like a completely different person!" Denis says.

He's right. The Ms. Sett who complains about everything from candy eating on Main Street to the growing number of local families who do yard work instead of church on Sunday mornings does not seem like this same woman.

"Maybe it's a different person," I say. "Like her mom or something."

Marci shakes her head. "It's her. She's just showing us the nice side today. I guarantee you there's more to this first-day routine than we can see right now."

Grandad packed me a peanut butter and jelly sandwich and a bag of fluorescent-orange cheese curls for lunch. I get my stuff set up and shake my bottle of chocolate milk.

"You can't have those!" Marci whispers, pointing at the cheese curls.

"I can have whatever I want."

"The school doesn't allow junk food," Marci says. "Ms. Sett has written about that repeatedly."

"Junk is a matter of perception," I say. "If she or anyone else has a problem with what my grandad packs for lunch, then they can take it up with him. I wish them luck. He's more stubborn than I am."

Denis says, "Your superpower is your bluntness."

I say, "Yes, it is."

Marci sighs. "I just don't want you to get in trouble." She's red in the face . . . but not from anything we've said. The cafeteria has hundreds of students in it and it's so humid, my cheese curls are going stale.

"I'm not getting in trouble," I assure Marci.

At the same time, I'll admit—I'm glad Ms. Sett isn't in the room as I chomp some Cheetos.

The rest of the day is easy. We have recess and then music before we get back to the classroom, where we all get divided up for math. Ms. Sett gives us homework on the first day of school—forty math problems.

Denis is breathing so deep everyone can hear him. Homework makes him irrationally upset. And being lied to makes him freak out completely.

Ms. Sett notices and smiles at Denis warmly. "I know I said this morning that you'd have very little homework," she tells him, "but that's once we get into the year's work. For now, we have to review and make sure you remember what you learned last year."

Denis calms down. I'm sure Ms. Sett already read the papers filed with the office about Denis's problems with homework. And his anxiety. And probably his fear of snakes and water. (And water snakes, which seems obvious.) Also, Denis is afraid of tongues. This sounds weird, but he can't even look at his own tongue in the mirror without feeling sick. I don't know if the school knows that.

I honestly don't mind that I've got to watch my tongue

when Denis is around. He's the best friend I've ever had. We're going to be friends until we're old and sitting on the benches on Main Street, me eating candy and him eating string cheese. Maybe he'll still be afraid of water snakes and his own tongue. Maybe not. I don't care as long as he's still the most loyal person I've ever met and he still talks to me.

I've been called unlikable.

I blame my parents, one of whom is a normal American mom who is full of grace, and the other who is a rabbit-fearing cranky alien from a planet three galaxies away called BD-134. How this makes me unlikable: Both of them encourage me to say what's on my mind.

Anyway, this is how it all starts: Me, Denis, and Marci in Ms. Sett's classroom. BOT DUCK MAN. Record-breaking hot autumn weather with no air-conditioning. Rules about girls wearing shorts. How your history books don't tell you the whole truth. How my dad says he's from BD-134. How everything seems so perfect on the first day of school. Too perfect.

Who Makes the Rules?

I moved here a year ago and I don't think people in this town realize how weird it is to have a rule against junk food. Who can say that a food is junk food? And what kind of person thinks they can rule over a whole town's eating habits? I also find it interesting that there are three candy stores in town.

—Sam Paris, New Street

Re: Who Makes the Rules?

Our town serves tourists, and candy stores are good business. That said, maybe Sam Paris has not noticed that our country has an obesity problem. Junk food is junk because it has little to no nutritional value and it is often overused as snack food. May I suggest you go to the farmers' market and note the wide array of fruits and vegetables available there.

—Laura Samuel Sett

Lit Circle

O n the Friday of our third week of the school year, Ms. Sett looks excited and smiles a lot. We've moved our desks into pods again, which feels a lot less like college and a lot more like kindergarten, but it's what we're used to and it helps for group work. Denis hasn't slouched in three whole weeks and Marci has stopped talking about women's rights during social studies class because we aren't learning history anymore, only geography.

Yesterday, Ms. Sett said Mexico was part of North America but "not quite the same as North America." I raised my hand to protest, but in three short weeks, she has learned to ignore my knack for discussing the truth of things.

Fact: Mexico is a bona fide part of North America.

Fact: There are three big, mysterious boxes on Ms. Sett's desk.

After a half-hour-long lesson on North American topography, which includes having to listen to Aaron James talk about how the Earth is flat for two minutes, arguing that the Rocky Mountains should cast shadows on the clouds above them if the Earth was really round, Ms. Sett finally walks to the boxes on her desk and opens them.

Note: She doesn't correct Aaron James, who says *the Earth is flat.*

"It's our first lit circle day," she says. "I've broken you into groups based on the titles you all chose—we'll have six novels and six groups!" She points to the board, clicks her remote control, and shows us our names broken up into six groups.

She continues, "The idea is to read the book together, silently, during lit circle time or at home, and discuss with one another after each chapter or section. There will be worksheets to make sure you're reading, vocabulary lists, and quizzes to make sure you're understanding what you read. The trick is to not read ahead." When she says this, she clicks the remote control again and a slide appears, black background and red letters—DON'T READ AHEAD!

Denis, Marci, and I land in the same group, which is

awesome. We all rush to the pod of tables that Ms. Sett said was for group six. Aaron is in group six, too. And Hannah Do, who usually stays very quiet on account of her being half the size of the biggest kid in the room, who also happens to be Aaron. Seeing Aaron and Hannah sit next to each other is like seeing a T. rex and a piece of bread sit next to each other.

"I don't even know what book I picked," Aaron says.

"I've read this book before," Hannah says. "It's good. You'll like it."

Aaron looks at the four of us and smirks. He thinks we're all losers for believing that Earth is round. I doubt he'll like any book.

Marci asks Hannah, "If you already read it, why'd you pick it?"

"I've read all of them before."

Marci nods. Denis sits up straight. I make a nervous cough. Aaron farts and doesn't say *excuse me*.

Ms. Sett moves from desk pod to desk pod, handing out books from her boxes. She comes to us last and hands each of us a copy of *The Devil's Arithmetic* by Jane Yolen. I'm relieved at how short it is, and the cover intrigues me. It says *Winner of the National Jewish Book Award* under the title, and under that is a yellow six-pointed star patch—the kind that Nazis made Jewish people wear to mark them during World War Two. I know right away the book is about the Holocaust and I wonder if Denis will feel sick when the Nazis in the book do Nazi things.

I also wonder how Aaron will react. Did he know what the book was about when he chose it, or did he think it was a book about satanic algebra problems? One time when we talked about going to the Air and Space Museum in Washington, DC, Denis said he wanted to see the moon lander, and Aaron told him that the moon landing was fake. I look at him now and wonder if he'll say the same about the Holocaust.

I try not to judge. Mom always says not to judge, and that no one knows the reality of another person. But looking at Aaron James and his smirk, I feel like something bad is going to happen in group six. I just don't know what it is yet.

The alarm bell rings for a fire drill, and we all leave our copies of *The Devil's Arithmetic* on our desks and march outside single file.

Classic timing.

During club block at the end of the day—Marci is off singing in chorus and Denis is at chess club—I pick up the novel again and start reading the opening pages. There is a word on the first page that I have to look up. Ms. Sett still makes us use old-style dictionaries. The definition of *Seder* is: a Jewish feast and related ceremony on the first night or nights of Passover. The definition of *Passover* is: the Jewish festival commemorating the Israelites' exodus from Egypt.

I write the answers down on the vocabulary worksheet, but have no real idea what they mean. My family doesn't have a religion, really. Grandad celebrates Easter, but only because of jelly beans and chocolate. We celebrate Christmas, but only the tree-and-Santa-Claus kind. I've never been to church, except one time for a spaghetti dinner to support Grandad's friends who fought in the Korean War. Religion never really interested me before, but for some reason, this book by Jane Yolen has me interested in learning more. In this case, I'm interested in what it was like to be Jewish at a time when it meant you were in serious danger. More danger than I can imagine.

It's so hard for me to wrap my mind around. The Holocaust was a Nazi Germany–sponsored genocide— mass murder—of Jewish people from 1941 to 1945. Six million European Jewish people died, which was two-thirds of the Jewish people in Europe. The Nazis and their allies also targeted other people—disabled people, gay people, European Roma people, political enemies—and murdered millions of them, too, but most of the people they killed were Jews. The Nazis built enormous camps called extermination or concentration camps—places where they would ship the people they captured by train. The Nazis invented large deadly gas chambers where they would take a group of people to have a shower, but sometimes when they got into the shower rooms, lethal gas came out of the showerheads and killed them. That's just one way they killed Jewish people and people from the other groups I mentioned. They had a lot of ways, but that way was the one they used on millions and millions of people.

I can't think of a more horrible thing, really. And the longer time goes on, the less we talk about it. But we can't pretend it didn't happen—because when you pretend a thing didn't happen, that means it can happen again.

Anyway, the rest of the questions on the worksheet are about the book cover and the description on the back. I'm about to start filling it out, but Denis walks back into the classroom and gives me a fist bump on his way to his chair, which means he beat an opponent at chess club. Then Marci comes in and waves at me, and I put the worksheet and the book in my backpack and zip it in.

I don't read ahead.

Not yet.

Black Rectangle

When I get home from school, Dad is in the garage working on Grandad's old car. It's a bazillion degrees in there because he never opens the garage door and he's welding. He's a day early—this is usually what we do on Saturdays. Then, sometimes, if he's in a good mood, he takes me for flights in it in the middle of the night.

I'm too tired to work on the "spacecraft" today. Mom is at work, so I plop myself on the couch and turn on my favorite anime. The one in my brain.

It's about a boy with an alien dad and how they fly around in a spacecraft a lot before the boy has to go to middle school. That sounds like a boring anime, but there are secret aliens *everywhere* and the boy and father have special powers. The boy can change history. The father can melt your whole body just by looking at you a certain way.

That's the way Dad looks at me when he wakes me up from my accidental nap on the couch an hour later.

"Have you been home long?" he asks.

"I don't know," I say.

"Can you help me in the garage?"

"Sure."

For the next thirty minutes, I help Dad fix the dashboard. I hear the phone ringing in the house, but I'm holding a piece in place while he tightens something underneath with what looks like a weird space wrench. When we're done, we cover it with a tarp and he leaves right before Mom gets home.

She thinks it's just a vintage car. Specifically a 1967 Volkswagen Karmann Ghia convertible. I don't ever tell her what Dad says because he made me promise not to.

Before he catches the bus to his apartment, Dad says, "Maybe we'll take a ride again soon!"

"But what about tomorrow?"

"Can't make it tomorrow until late, sport. Something came up."

"Oh."

"Doesn't mean I don't love ya!" he says, and walks down the sidewalk.

Fact: Aliens lie. All the time. I can't find grace for that yet, but I'm trying.

When I come inside, Mom tells me, "Marci called and wants you to call her back and have your book with you." She's making dinner and has a wooden spoon in one hand and a spatula in the other.

"Which book?" I ask while I wash the grease off my hands.

"Something about a circle?" she says. "*Lit circle book.* That's what she called it. Can you set the table?"

I set the table but don't get the book. I'll call Marci back after we eat.

Over dinner, Mom asks what book we're reading, and I tell her. Then I say, "It's about the Holocaust."

"Tough topic," Mom says.

"Damn tough topic," my grandad says.

Mom scolds him for cursing.

Things get quiet at the table.

Grandad adds, "I've been to the camps. You can barely breathe there, even half a century later. Horrible. And I know horrible." Grandad served two tours in the Vietnam War and has a Purple Heart medal. He knows horrible.

We go on eating and Mom tells us a little about her

day. She's developing a new program for grieving kids and she has her last campfire group next week—they make s'mores and sing songs, and she says she loves every minute of it.

"I'm proud of you," Grandad says.

"Just doing my job," Mom replies.

"You help a hundred people every week. Just take the compliment, okay? Your mom would back me up on this," he says, laughing.

Mom smiles at him and then me, and then the three of us get up and clear the table and load the dishwasher.

When I call Marci back after dinner, I don't bring the book.

"I left a detailed message to save us time," she says.

"It's a Friday night. Who cares about time?"

"When you see what I'm about to tell you, you'll understand."

I walk to my backpack in the hallway and get the book. I roll my eyes the whole time. Leave it to Marci to expect efficiency on the weekend. "Got it."

"Open to page ninety-three."

I do. And I see it right away. "Oh."

There is an ugly black rectangle over some words.

"I talked to Hannah an hour ago and her book has

the same stuff. Go to page one hundred seventeen," she says.

I turn the pages. There's another ugly black rectangle over more words.

"The library opens at ten tomorrow," Marci says. "Want to meet me there?"

I'm still staring at the black rectangles. I thumb through to see if I can find any more places that are like it, but this is it—two areas of the book that are blacked out so well that the ink bleeds through to the other side. "Why would anyone do this?" I ask Marci.

"I don't know," she says.

"It's even the winner of the National Jewish Book Award!"

"Yeah," she says. "Whoever did this has some nerve."

"I mean, it's not like a kids' book would have anything that bad in it, you know?"

"Read around the black parts," she says. "Can you figure it out?"

Page 93 is a really hard page to read. It's a scene in the showers at a concentration camp. There are girls our age there and they're naked in the shower room. Surrounding them are Nazi soldiers. When the water turns off, the soldiers yell at the naked girls to move. When they move to the next room, they aren't given clothes to wear and are freezing. Even with a few words crossed out, it's a terrifying scene and my stomach hurts.

Page 117 is harder to figure out. I'm not sure what the scene is about, but it has something to do with little children having to hide in enormous piles of garbage at the concentration camp. Disgusting but not as terrifying as the shower scene.

I say, "I can't figure it out. What could be worse than this scene?"

"I don't know," Marci says. "But tomorrow, I'm going to find out."

"I'll meet you at the library at ten."

"Bring Denis," she says.

"Why?"

She sighs hard. "Because we're all best friends since first grade and I think he should be there."

"Best friends?"

"Yeah," she says.

When Mom first told me about grace and how to use it, she said never to agree with anything important that isn't true. But I can't figure out if what Marci said isn't true.

Library

No matter who tells you it's cool, there is no reason to be in a library early on a Saturday morning. No matter how beautiful your library is, no matter if it has old, tall columns, no matter if it was once part of a Revolutionary War hospital.

It's not that I don't like appearing smart or interested in books—I am both smart and interested in books. It's the fact that it's ten o'clock in the morning. Most kids up this early on a Saturday are practicing a sport or helping a parent at the grocery store, or even doing one of Sage Jones's poetry-pottery workshops where you can make a teacup and saucer with your own haiku glazed into them.

I don't think I've ever seen Marci Thompson on a weekend before. Denis looks just as sleepy as I do as he walks up the hill to the library. He shoots a glance at me, and all I can think to do is shrug.

There are so many babies here, with tired moms and dads, standing in front of a sign that reads INFANT STORY TIME! 10:15 A.M. SATURDAY! We let them go first once the doors are opened. Then the three of us step inside.

Marci says, "Come on," and dives into the children's section. She braves three babies—one who's crying over a picture of a pumpkin in a book—and finds the Y shelf for fiction. There are five Jane Yolen books on the shelf, but none are *The Devil's Arithmetic*.

"I'll ask if they can get it from another library," she says, and goes to stand in line at the front desk. Denis thumbs through a book about woodworking, and I watch a baby drool down its mom's back. The string measures at least two feet—impressive.

By the time Marci, Denis, and I are walking out of the library, it's 10:08 a.m. We don't have the book, and we don't have anything else to do.

"Hey," Denis says, "why don't we try the bookstore?"

"I don't have any money," Marci says.

"We can just look at the book, not buy it," I point out.

Marci says, "Oh! That's smart!"

"I have four dollars in quarters," Denis informs us. "I

was going to ask if you guys wanted to go feed the ducks in the park after the library." The ducks don't eat the quarters. There are machines with duck food at the park because it's not good to feed ducks bread.

"Great idea, Denis!" Marci says.

I feel a weird kind of jealousy that makes no sense. Grandad warned me about this. He wasn't trying to be weird, but he told me to be careful being friends with girls at my age because I might "feel things." Fact: I feel like a jerk for not bringing quarters, too.

Dress Codes Are Outdated!

My daughter has been sent home three times for "dress code violations" except that she wasn't violating dress code. This fall is very warm and she wore shorts to school. Shorts are an acceptable thing to wear in a school—especially when the air-conditioning is old or out of order. Boys are allowed to wear shorts. This policy is wrong and something should be done about it.

—Gretchen Good, Main Street

Re: Dress Codes Are Outdated!

Unless you work in a school as I do, you cannot see the value in a strict dress code. Boys become distracted by the littlest things as it is. The last thing we need is for them to be more distracted. Use your common sense! No one was wearing shorts in the 1800s and they didn't complain!

—Laura Samuel Sett

Tad's Books

Tad's Books on Main Street is the perfect place for a cool nerd like me. It has the best collection of manga and a whole shelf of books about Dungeons & Dragons. It's wall-to-wall, floor-to-ceiling books—every kind of book, too. From cookbooks to helicopter pilot manuals to books of love poems Grandad would like. Tad's is also full of board games, and over winter, Grandad and I go to game night there and play all different stuff with whoever shows up. Sometimes it's old people or random adults, and sometimes it's kids my age, like Denis.

No one is named Tad, by the way. Tad is a mix of the original owners' names—Tony, Ann, and David. I think they're all dead now. Grandad knew Tony Farisi and he always uses the same word to talk about him:

sanctimonious. When I asked him why he always uses that word, he said, "He owned a bookstore and I was all over the place with PTSD from the war. About fifteen years after I got back, you know? I mixed up the names of two rivers in France. He never let me forget it. Sanctimonious turd."

Turd is a word old people use instead of a curse word. *Sanctimonious* means *smug*. *Smug*, which is one of my favorite words, means *superior*. PTSD is post-traumatic stress disorder, and it can mean a lot of things, but for Grandad it means he had some trouble adjusting after he came back from the Vietnam War.

I know my way around Tad's Books, so it's easy to find a used copy of *The Devil's Arithmetic* while Marci and Denis are drawn to the new release table. I skip to page 93 to find out what was so bad that someone had to black it out in our school copies.

I find it.

I read it.

I read it again.

The whole scene—the Nazi soldiers and the young girls in the concentration camp shower and how naked and cold they were and how the Nazi guards were standing right there with big guns and screaming at them to move . . . it's such a hard scene and it really shows how scary and impossible it all was.

I read the phrase again.

I shake my head.

Marci and Denis come over and I sigh. "You guys aren't going to believe this," I say. "I don't even know how to tell you."

I hold the book out. I point to the sentence. *Head down, hands over her breasts, Hannah walked through the line of soldiers . . .*

Marci reads it once, then reads it again. Denis reads it and frowns.

Marci holds her school copy of the book up for comparison.

Head down, ██████████████████ Hannah walked through the line of soldiers . . .

Marci says, "Breasts?" and the three other people shopping at Tad's look over and then go back to browsing books. "They censored the word *breasts?* Are you kidding me?"

"In that scene, too. I mean, wow." I feel dumb for not being able to say anything more daring or definitive.

Marci almost yells it this time. "*BREASTS!* Seriously?"

Greg, the manager of Tad's, comes over. "What're you guys up to?"

Denis shows him our school copy. "They censored our reading book," he says. "About the Holocaust."

"Oh. I love that book," Greg says. "And who's *they*?"

"We don't know yet," I tell him. "They crossed out the word *breasts*—as if we don't know what breasts are."

"What grade are you guys in again?" Greg asks.

"Sixth," Marci answers. "Old enough to have *actual* breasts, so I don't understand the problem."

Greg nods. "People can be weird."

"Especially in this town," Denis says.

"Guys," I say. "My tongue is all twisted in my mouth and I can't see right. I think I'm going to pass out." I stumble a little. Greg steadies my elbow. "It's the word. It's just not right for me to read. It's just not . . ."

Marci and Denis and Greg all look like they're about to call 911. So I stop and say, "Just kidding. Trying to make a point."

Sometimes cool-nerd funny is not easy to understand. Grandad warned me about that, too.

We look up the other passage that's crossed out. Page 117.

Marci says, "Wow." She points to the book.

Denis and I lean in to read. Page 117 has a scene where the older girls are explaining to the main character something about how the little kids have to hide in garbage dumps when the Commandant comes to the concentration camp to visit. One girl is explaining how the older girls don't have to do this, but how she is assumed older even though she may not look it physically.

She motioned toward her own undeveloped chest.

That's what's crossed out in our books. ██████████ ████████████████████████ The whole sentence— gone.

"Undeveloped chest," I say.

Greg the manager says, "That's just weird."

Denis says, "Whoever censored this book has something against basic human anatomy."

Marci says, "Whoever censored this book has something wrong with their brain."

I say, "We have to find out who did this."

"It's like they think we're stupid," Denis says.

"They do think we're stupid," Marci says.

Greg nods, but then has to go wait on a customer.

By this time, more weekend shoppers have come in. Mostly tourists. As they look at me and see a sixth-grade kid, I wonder what words they would cross out to protect me.

"How do we find out who did this?" Marci asks.

"I don't know," I reply. "But we should start with Ms. Sett."

Denis says, "I wonder why she'd do this to books, though. She loves books."

It's true. Ms. Sett can't stop talking about how much she loves books, and her classroom library is the biggest I've ever seen.

"I told you she isn't what she seems like in school," Marci says.

The question is: If that's true, what can we do about it?

The Mug

B y the time I get back home, Mom and Grandad have weeded and mulched the flower beds and pruned all the plants and bushes around our yard. It's like we're closing the house down for fall and eventually winter—but it's still shorts-and-T-shirt weather.

Grandad says it's unnatural for it to be this hot in October.

"By the time I'm your age," I tell Grandad, "they say the climate in Pennsylvania will be like northern Arkansas."

"It already feels it," Mom says, wiping sweat from her forehead. "Let's get some lunch."

"I have to take a quick shower. I stink!" Grandad proclaims. Mom laughs and he walks to his side door.

Mom and I go inside.

"How about a ham and cheese sandwich?" she asks. "I have potato salad."

I say yes and I ask her as I set the table, "So did you ever have to read a book that was censored?"

"You mean banned books?"

"I don't know," I say. "I think?"

"I've read many banned books. A lot of books have been banned, though."

"Huh. Why?" I ask.

"People are scared of them, I guess."

"I don't get it."

"Have you seen my blue mug?" Mom asks, her head in the mugs-and-glasses cabinet.

"No," I answer. "Why would anyone be afraid of a book? There are guns and snakes and all kinds of other stuff for sale that could actually kill you."

Mom brings food to the table. I go to fill water glasses. When I open the mugs-and-glasses cabinet, I have an extra look for her blue mug. It's her favorite. Gram gave it to her.

"They're afraid of the ideas, Mac. You know. Same as the watchdogs for candy and girls' knees. Some people just think everyone should think like them. Or be like them."

Grandad arrives in the middle of Mom's answer. "What are we talking about?"

I say, "Censorship."

"In what way?" he asks.

"Banned books," Mom says.

"I *love* banned books. I used to read as many to you as I could when you were little, Mac."

"You read me banned books?" I say this sarcastically because I know he's making it up.

"Almost exclusively," he answers—dead serious. "*Charlotte's Web* and the poetry book by—uh—Silverstein—uh."

"*Where the Sidewalk Ends*?" I say.

"And Reynolds—brave . . . uh . . ."

"*As Brave as You?* No! How could anyone ban that?"

"Yeah. And Paterson's *Bridge to Terabithia*. Remember that one?"

"I cried for a whole day."

Mom says, "*Where the Wild Things Are. And Tango Makes Three. Melissa.*"

"Captain Underpants!" Grandad adds.

"A lot of younger books you loved. *I Am Rosa Parks*," Mom says. "And *Last Stop on Market Street* and *Henry's Freedom Box*, and . . ."

Grandad says, *"Roll of Thunder, Hear My Cry!"*

It's like a banned books game show. I had no idea that my entire childhood was made up of books that other people didn't think I should read.

"Hey, Dad, did you use my blue mug and forget to return it?" Mom asks.

"I never use it," he says, shaking his head. "I know what it means to you."

The two of them look a certain way when they think of Gram. It's not entirely sad. It's not happy, either. It's a sort of look that means something good happened and that good thing is over now, but isn't it nice we have the memories? I remember Gram. I was only seven when she died. She smelled like cinnamon all the time and made the best crumb cake in the world.

"Where'd you go off to this morning?" Grandad asks me.

"Adventures with Denis and Marci," I tell him. "The library and then the bookstore and then the park to feed ducks because we were bored."

"The library?" Mom says.

"Who says I can't go to the library on a Saturday?"

Mom looks at me suspiciously.

"Where's Mike?" Grandad asks. Mike is my dad.

"He can't be here until later," Mom says.

"Oh yeah," I say.

Mom says, "He's going to bring me more of those squashes."

"Your squash soup." Grandad makes a gesture like he's kissing soup. Then he looks at me and leans forward, into my face. "Why were you at the library on a Saturday morning? And why are you talking about banned books? And if you weren't at the library, you can tell us where you were. We won't turn you in."

This makes all three of us laugh. I take a huge bite of my sandwich and smile as I chew. And chew. And chew. It was a big bite.

"I think I'm the one who brought up banned books," Mom says.

I nod. Chew more. And more. Until it's finally wash-it-back-with-milk time.

I say, "I have to show you something."

I get up and grab my school copy of *The Devil's Arithmetic*. I tell them what's going on. They both keep touching the black Sharpie rectangles as if there's texture there. Mom looks serious.

"Breasts?"

"Yep."

"Sixth grade?"

"Yep."

"Breasts?" Mom says again. Shakes her head. Has a look on her face I can't quite describe.

Grandad asks, "Did you buy the copy you found at Tad's?"

"We only had enough money for duck food."

"Let's take a walk after lunch," Grandad says. "I want to see it."

Of course Grandad buys me the copy of *The Devil's Arithmetic* at Tad's. We walk through the park, and then up and around the cemetery. When we get home, we play a game of backgammon. He always wins. After he wins, he always takes a nap.

I look through the new book and read page 93 again. The scene is still terrifying—the Nazi guards, the freezing-cold showers, the girls—and Jane Yolen does such a great job showing how bad things were, and how weird. Like— surreal, you know? How could anyone believe that was even happening? The Holocaust was so bad, it's hard to really understand it. The scene, without the black rectangle, with all the words in the right place, feels real now. It's the truth. That's the point. Jane Yolen wanted us to read the truth—every single word of it.

I am just like her, which is why I ask questions on field trips about how many of the signers of the Declaration of Independence owned slaves. Because most of my school and this town is populated by white people—like 97 percent of it—we rarely talk about stuff like this. It's seen as too serious or too sensitive or even impolite, and some people think that it will make white kids feel bad, but if we want to change the world so it's good for everyone, it's important to talk about the truth.

I think about Dad and wonder what his truth is. Sometimes I think we're just an anthropology project to him. Sometimes I fear he's going to fix his ship and disappear without saying goodbye. I check the garage while Grandad is napping and the ship is still there, under its cover.

Action Station

After dinner, Mom has her laptop open as she sits in her favorite chair, and Grandad has a legal pad and his favorite pen. (It works underwater, he says, but we've never tested it.)

Mom says, "Most of the stuff I'm finding has to do with really banning books—like removing them from the school. This kind of censorship, blacking out words, either isn't common or it's not usually reported, I guess."

"That's how it gets done," Grandad says.

"I think we want to do this ourselves," I say. "I mean, I appreciate the help, but Marci and Denis and I will figure it out."

"I'm not going to do it for you," Mom says. "But you have to understand that we care about this stuff."

"Do you know what the school taxes cost around here?" Grandad says. "We paid for those books!"

"Good point, Dad," Mom says. "Write that down."

Grandad writes it down.

"Okay," I say. "But we really want to do this ourselves, I think."

Grandad smiles at me. "Don't worry, kid. We won't step on your toes."

I hear the garage door open and close. Dad arrives through the garage doorway with two butternut squashes in his hands. He stands in the living room, looking at us and our action station—two legal pads, pens, Mom on her computer, and a few banned children's books that I got from my bookshelf in my room. I look up and wave.

"Are you three running for president?" he asks.

"Something like that," Grandad says, head down, still writing. "How was your week, Mike?"

Dad puts the squashes on the countertop in the kitchen. "Pretty good. Sorry I'm late."

Grandad just nods and keeps writing on the legal pad.

Mom says, "I saved dinner for you. It's on a plate in the fridge."

"Thanks," Dad says, and gets up to reheat it.

While Mom and Grandad keep researching and writing, I

open up my school copy of *The Devil's Arithmetic* and stare at the black rectangles. I move to the kitchen table—not because Dad would be eating alone if I didn't but because I need to write something down. I pick up my school computer, log in, and search for Jane Yolen's website. Once I find her CONTACT page, I start typing in the spot where you can write to her.

Dear Ms. Yolen,

Dad asks, "Is there any soda in the house?"
Mom says, "Sorry, no."
Dad reaches for a glass and fills it with water.

I am writing to you from Pennsylvania. I go to Independence North Elementary School and we are reading your book, *The Devil's Arithmetic*, in our lit circle class. It's a really great book and I'm learning a lot.

"It's going to get hotter next week," Dad says. "I can't believe it!"
Grandad says, "Yup."
Mom closes her laptop and puts it on the coffee table. She walks over to Dad and hands him a napkin. "Good to see you," she says.

He nods and says, "Same here." After a few moments, he says to me, "Sorry I missed our day, kid. Something came up."

"Sure," I say. I hate to admit it, but I forgot about Dad and the spaceship. I had things to do, I guess.

I knew about the Holocaust before I read your book, but the way you show it here makes it very real and I can feel the fear of the people who had to live through it. What a horrible and terrifying story. It's almost impossible to believe that people did that to other people.

Mom goes to the kitchen area—our living room and kitchen are one big room, really—and looks into the fridge. "Mac, can you add sour cream to the store list?"

I'm still typing my letter, so Dad grabs a pencil and the pad from the table and adds it.

"And I should probably get more eggs," Mom adds. "I'm baking a crumb cake this week." That's Dad's favorite cake, but he doesn't say anything. He just adds eggs to the list.

Mom starts to empty the dishwasher.

"Oh, hey, Mike, have you seen my blue mug anywhere?"

Dad shovels food into his mouth like he's suddenly ravenous. I watch him chew and then I go back to typing.

But I'm writing to you today because we are having a
problem here with censorship. I'm not sure who, but
someone crossed out a few words in our copies of your
book. I wanted you to know that because I think it
would be great to have your support as my friends and
I try to fight our school to get new copies of the book that

"Mike?" Mom asks.

"Yeah?" Dad answers.

"Have you seen my blue mug anywhere?"

A few beats go by while Dad finishes chewing. "I
smashed it," he answers, a blob of food in his cheek.

He offers nothing more. No explanation or description. He knows why that mug is important.

"Oh," Mom says. "Okay. Like, you accidentally broke it?"

"No," he says.

"Oh," Mom says.

Grandad is suddenly standing behind me.

don't have the words crossed out. So first I want to tell
you what they crossed out. I can't tell you why yet
because we haven't found out who did it yet. But our
teacher is kinda famous in this town for making rules
about stuff, so I have a feeling it was her.

"How'd it break?" Grandad asks.

"I smashed it. I told you," Dad says.

"On purpose?" Mom asks.

Dad sighs. Not like he's sorry, but like he's annoyed. "I was really angry, okay?"

Mom's eyebrows move down to the place where she thinks best.

Grandad is still behind me and I can hear him taking long, deep breaths.

"Did you know what mug it was when you smashed it?" Mom asks.

"Yeah," Dad answers.

"Oh," Mom says. She looks at Grandad. The air in the house is suddenly thin. I can't seem to breathe right.

Grandad puts his hand on my arm and rubs it gently. "Wanna go for a night walk?" he asks.

"No," I say. Because I'm tired of leaving Mom here on Saturday nights to fend for herself. She helps people all week long. She makes crumb cakes and the best soup, and makes dinner for Dad every Saturday for his visit, and half the time he's a jerk to her.

Grandad keeps his hand on my arm.

"So you smashed a really important thing of mine and knew you were smashing it and you can't even apologize?"

Mom says. "I don't mean to scold you, but that's not nice."

"I was angry. I told you."

"That's not right, Dad." That's what I say. I know what's right and what isn't.

He ignores me.

Grandad keeps deep breathing behind me. Mom's eyebrows are still down, but now in that place where they sit when Mom cries.

"She can't ever replace something like that," Grandad says.

"I'll get her a new one," Dad says. "Plenty of pottery stores in town sell blue mugs. Sorry."

I go back to writing my letter.

But someone crossed out the word "breasts" in your book, Ms. Yolen. Even that part when she "motioned toward her own undeveloped chest." Can you even believe that? It's just stupid and wrong and I hate that we have to fight this because no one should have done it in the first place.

It sounds mad. And I am mad. But not at Jane Yolen.

I just don't understand why adults want to lie to kids. Or to anybody. I'm sitting in my house right now and my dad is lying to my mom about how he's "sorry" that he smashed her favorite blue mug because he was mad. He doesn't even care that he seems scary or weird. He's just acting like it's no big deal, the same as I suspect the school will act when we bring them your book and the censored words.

To be honest, I'm a little scared to go to the school about this. I just don't have a good feeling about adults around here and their ability to tell the whole truth.

I will keep you posted.

Sincerely,
Mac Delaney

When I finish, I look up and Dad grins at me. That makes me look down again.

And then he is suddenly really mad at all of us.

"Why are you guys always ganging up on me?" he says. "I'm trying, okay? I come every Saturday like we agreed, okay?"

Mom has her back to us and is standing in front of the stove. I don't see her shaking and don't hear her sniffling, so I don't think she's crying. I would be. I nearly am. That mug is why I know so many stories about Gram.

I want to blurt out the truth. *Dad doesn't think he's from Earth. He doesn't understand feelings of sentimentality or how a blue mug can mean more than a blue mug.* None of it comes out of my mouth. I don't know why my first instinct is to defend him.

"I—I'm, um—" That's all I can say.

I'm trying to find enough grace jam to pretend like this isn't happening. Sometimes jam is sweet, like when Aaron tells people at recess that the moon landing was fake and I can ignore him. But sometimes jam is sticky and hard to wipe off. Like when it lands on your shirt and dries. That's the kind of jam I am right now. Forced grace. All sticky.

Dad looks at me and grins again a little like it's funny I can't find words.

"Come with me, Mac," Grandad says.

I know his tone and I don't argue. I save a copy of my letter to Jane Yolen onto my desktop, hit SUBMIT, then close the computer. Grandad tells me to put a sweatshirt on. I grab my Todoroki sweatshirt from the hall. We go for a night walk.

Usually we talk on our night walks. This time, we don't.

I don't even know what to say anymore. Part of me wants to tell Grandad that I just sent a letter to an author without even proofreading it and I feel stupid. But I'm kinda glad I sent the letter. I'm sure she gets all kinds of letters from kids who don't proofread.

We end up at the small park with the creek running through it. It's after hours, so we're not allowed to be there. We sit on a bench by the creek for a while. It's a memorial bench for a girl who died a few years ago. It says YOU'RE BEAUTIFUL on it. I try to feel beautiful but I'm keeping too many secrets.

"Dad isn't like us," I say to Grandad.

"Ain't that the truth."

"I mean he's not from here. He's—it's like he's from somewhere else."

"Oh?" Grandad says.

"Yeah. He doesn't have feelings like we have."

"That's a good trick. I wish I didn't have feelings some-times," Grandad says. "But he seems to have plenty of angry, don't you think?"

We sit and listen to the running water for a while. Grandad gets his meditation beads out of his pocket and closes his eyes and considers each bead with his fingers as he breathes. I feel wrong watching him, but it's amazing how he can relax his face, and when he does, he smiles a little. As if his natural facial state is smiling.

"I can feel you looking at me," he says. "I can teach you how to do this, you know."

"It's fine," I say. "My brain is too fast. I even think while I'm thinking about other stuff."

"Okay," he says, and keeps breathing and smiling.

"It looks peaceful, though."

He nods.

When we get back to the house, Mom is reading one of her favorite poetry books under a blanket Gram knitted. Grandad gives her a kiss on the top of her head like she's twelve.

"Your dad will come by on Friday after school," she says. "He says he has to pay you back for missing today."

"He doesn't have to pay me back for today." He's my dad, right? Not a customer in a store.

"He'll be here Friday and Saturday. Already put in his order for dinner both nights," she says. "Six o'clock, like always." Her voice is calm and kind. I have no idea how, after everything that just happened.

I guess she knows much more about grace than I do.

Things You Don't Expect

No one expects a spaceship. No one *ever* expects a spaceship. I guess this is why Dad and I only take rides in the middle of the night.

It's one in the morning. I'm sleeping but he comes up to my room and whispers "Let's roll!" into my ear, same way as always, and tells me to get ready. Space is cold, so even though it's still hot out, he tells me to wear warm clothes.

We open the garage door quietly and push the craft into the alley, roll it while Dad gets in and starts it, and then I jump in and we fly over Independence North Elementary School, and up over all the stores on Main Street and past the flagpole and the train car in the park and over the fire station and up the highway to the shopping mall and the fast-food restaurants on the outskirts of town.

There is a twenty-four-hour McDonald's here, and Dad pulls into the drive-through lane. I order something sweet, with no nutritional value, and we take off into orbit and watch the Earth below us. Only a few people know what Earth looks like from up here. Aaron James would really be disappointed to find out how round Earth is. Marci would probably cry at how beautiful it is. Denis would be nervous but try not to show it. Dad and I eat junk food. In the middle of the night. After he was a jerk to us. As if this is completely normal.

"So what was happening when I came in tonight? You all looked busy," he says.

"My reading book from school is censored and I don't know what to do about it," I say to him.

"Censored how?"

"Someone crossed out two lines of text with a black marker."

"What do they say?"

"Both refer to breasts or girls' chests," I answer.

Dad chuckles through his nose and I think about why I'm even here with him. I was sleeping and got up in a daze. I don't even want to be here.

"What does Denis think?"

"Denis is too worried about the possible existence of

extended-stay botflies," I say. "But I guess he just wants to find out why whoever censored the books did it."

Dad crumples up his Big Mac wrapper and tosses it back in the brown bag. "I think we all know who censored the books and why. And there isn't any such thing as an extended-stay botfly. Good guess, though."

"He's got a bug bite from last summer that won't go away, is all," I say. "He says he can't see any movement under his skin, but then, sometimes, he says he swears he feels something is in there."

"I know. And it's not a botfly. It's a species from a few galaxies away. If it's still in his leg now, for a whole year, it's probably due to hatch soon. Don't worry. One day he'll wake up and it will be gone and it will be a mystery."

"Oh," I say. "What happens after it hatches?"

"It'll grow into a cat."

I don't know what to say. I want it to be a joke. But Dad isn't laughing.

"If you need to know," he says, "domesticated cats are not from Earth. Wild cats aren't even from Earth. They aren't spies as much as they're anthropologists, like me. They watch and report back—write articles in magazines about humans and stuff."

"Like *National Geographic*?"

"Yes. Like that," he answers.

"Do you write any of those articles?" I ask.

"I *contribute*," he says. "Usually I'm more of an on-the-ground research guy. I'm who they call to make sure they have their facts straight."

"And *they* is the cats who make magazines like *National Geographic* but about humans?"

"Yes."

"Are you really my father?"

"Yes."

"So is that even allowed? You, um, having babies with humans?"

"No."

"Did you do it so you could be an on-the-ground research assistant?" I ask.

"I did it because I was interested in learning about love," Dad says. "Humans have this pull toward each other. They have the opposite, too, of course. Hate is equally interesting. But I wanted to study love, you see. Then I met your mother."

"And you loved her?"

"She loved me," he says. "I can't love like humans love." That stings. "Oh."

"Not romantic love, anyway. But I can love you. I do love you. It's the most enthralling feeling I have ever felt. Like I won the biggest prize."

I feel warm anger rising in my chest. I'm a person, not a prize.

He revs the engine and we fly back through town, low over the park, and we scare the ducks who were sleeping under the trees. Some of them fly up in protest, and Dad laughs and quacks at them. Two people walking on Main Street see us and point. I wave because what does it matter that we're in a spacecraft and I still have a McDonald's chocolate milkshake. It's two in the morning and tomorrow is Sunday and Grandad and I will take our Sunday walk and he'll name all the trees and tell me about what it was like to fight in a war or protest for civil rights.

We get closer to the house, and Dad lands the spacecraft and drives slowly home.

"Did you really smash Mom's mug on purpose?"

"Yep."

"That's really bad," I say.

"I was angry. I couldn't control myself." *Now* he's smiling. Like this is a joke.

"I mean—I guess—I mean that you shouldn't have smashed Mom's mug."

"She'll get over it. Earth women have to cry awhile before they feel better. That's all."

He kills the engine before we get to the house and we push it the rest of the way, like always. Then I sneak upstairs and get back into bed. The clock says I've only been gone an hour but it felt like five. Not in a good way.

I can't fall back to sleep right away, so I grab my laptop and reread the letter I sent to Jane Yolen. At least there aren't any misspelled words. Part of me regrets telling her all that stuff about the mug. But I know I can't do anything about it and at least it's the truth.

Fall Play Inappropriate

I am concerned about the choice for our fall play. The play is *Girls Like That*, and while I understand that the school is private and all-girls and this material is relevant, I don't think teenagers should be talking about these issues. —Lois K., Spruce Street

Re: Fall Play Inappropriate

No plays mentioning any topic that is deemed "adult content" should be performed in this town. If people want to see that sort of thing, they can go to the next town. —Laura Samuel Sett

It's a private school. Take it up with them.

—John Cope, Newport Road

Why are we shutting out culture in this town? How does a play equate to a bag of Cheetos? I've lived here my whole life and I'm starting to get sick of the restrictions. Not to mention that *Girls Like That* is about a naked picture of a girl getting passed around a school, which is exactly what happened in the high school last year. Grow up! —Pat Z., Front Street

The Plan

Marci, Denis, and I go to the main office first thing on Monday and stand outside. None of us knows how to make an appointment with the principal but it seems like it should be easy. She's in the same building as us, for one thing, and we're her students, so she should be excited to talk to us.

"We should talk to the secretary," Denis says.

"As soon as possible so we can see her today," Marci adds.

Denis nods.

"Who's going to do it?" I ask.

They look at me.

So I go into the office and ask the secretary if I can make an appointment to see the principal today. "It's for three of us—me, Denis, and Marci," I explain.

She's looking at her computer screen. "Sixth grade, right?"

"Yep."

"How about just after lunch?"

That's recess, but I don't mind.

"Sure. That's perfect," I say.

"Great! She'll see you here at ten after twelve."

I say thank you and then walk with Marci and Denis to Ms. Sett's room.

"The first step is finding out who did it," I say.

"Then why they did it," Denis says.

"Then we fight it," Marci says.

Ms. Sett is outside her classroom door giving high fives and fist bumps to welcome everyone. Part of me still feels wrong for going over her head and going to the principal first, but the three of us agreed it would be best.

"Good morning, three musketeers," Ms. Sett says. "I hope you had a great weekend!"

"We did!" Marci replies.

Denis smiles. I feel like a liar because my weekend was . . . complicated. No one knows this except for me. I aim to keep it that way.

■

By the time lunch comes, Denis is nervous and jiggling his leg.

"Don't worry," I tell him. "She's going to be nice."

Marci says, "She's always nice!"

Denis jiggles his leg anyway and we wait for the bell to sound and slowly walk to the main office. We wait for a few minutes and then the secretary tells us we can go in. We say hi and sit down in the chairs in front of Dr. McKenny's desk. There's a handmade desk plate with an apple drawn on it that reads DR. PEGGY MCKENNY, PRINCIPAL.

"So," she says while giving us a double thumbs-up. "What can I do for you three?"

Marci pulls out her copy of *The Devil's Arithmetic*. "In two areas of this book, the words have been censored."

Dr. McKenny looks at the two pages Marci has marked with Post-it notes. "Whoever crossed this out sure meant it!" she says. "I'll get you a new copy, Marci."

"Ours have the same crossed-out words," I say. "All the copies are blacked out that way."

This clearly surprises Dr. McKenny. "Huh," she says.

"Do you know who might have done this?" Marci asks.

All of us, including Dr. McKenny, stay quiet because it

feels obvious—Ms. Sett writes all those letters and makes all those rules. But we have to make sure, I guess.

"I'm sure it's nothing," Dr. McKenny says. "It's only a few words."

"The word is *breast*," Marci says, "and it's not nothing. It's an insult to our intellectual freedom."

I'm impressed. Denis looks at his feet.

"As a taxpayer, my mom paid for those books," I say. "And this weekend we had to buy a replacement so I could read the book as it was meant to be read, not in a censored way that someone else thinks I should read."

"I'm sure it's just a mix-up," Dr. McKenny tells us. "No one wants to take any of your freedoms away. Or waste your mom's tax money, Mac."

Very hesitantly, Denis adds, "I don't mean to be disrespectful, but you seem to be acting like this isn't a problem. This is a problem. All the books have been censored. This is not just a mix-up. Someone did it on purpose."

"Please don't treat us like we don't know what we're talking about," Marci adds, the whole time staring shyly at Denis. "We've spent the entire weekend researching what to do when a school restricts our right to read. We know there should be a protocol when someone challenges a book. We know that we can protest like the students did down in York." York, Pennsylvania, just over the river, has been in the national news more than once for censoring things.

"Just because we're twelve doesn't mean we're dumb," I say.

Dr. McKenny sits back in her fancy leather desk chair and smiles and nods. "I'm so proud of you guys," she says. "Good for you for being so smart and using resources and planning how to fix this problem."

"So you didn't know these books were censored?" Marci asks.

"No. But I'll find out who did it and we'll go from there," Dr. McKenny answers.

"We all need new books," I say. "Greg at Tad's Books said he'd be happy to order however many you need."

Dr. McKenny puts her hands up and says, "Whoa, guys! Slow down. I'm sure this is all going to be fine." She keeps talking but it sounds like *blah-blah-blah* to me because I realize she's still pretending like this is okay. I can see it in her face. She's smiling in that way adults do when they think kids are doing something cute.

Fact: Being treated like a child makes me angry.

Fact: Being angry makes me scared that I might be like my dad.

On our walk back to class, I don't tell Marci or Denis that I don't trust Dr. McKenny. I pretend along with them that she's going to get to the bottom of the mystery and replace the censored books. I pretend she cares about the truth.

By Wednesday, Marci gets impatient.

"I don't know why it would take this long to find out who censored the books." She walks up the steps to the second floor and rounds the corner to go up the next flight. "We're all in the same building, right? It can't take that long to ask."

Marci must be mad, because she can usually go fast up these stairs and seem fine, but now she's breathing heavy. When she frowns, there's a dimple on her cheek that comes out, and even though I don't want her to frown, the dimple is, well, cute.

Anyway.

In the two days since our meeting, we've already read the first three chapters of *The Devil's Arithmetic* in lit circle and completed the worksheets Ms. Sett gave us. The story is about a girl named Hannah and what happens to her during Passover Seder. I don't want to spoil anything in the book, but it's not a historical novel, like you'd think due to the scenes that are censored and the subject matter. It's really a time-travel story—my favorite kind. Time travel is something I think about a lot because sometimes I feel like I was born at the wrong place in history.

I should have been born at a time when adults didn't pretend something is okay when it's not. I don't know if that time ever existed.

Maybe I needed to be born in the future.

The B-Word

At recess on Wednesday, while Marci still talks about how Dr. McKenny should have gotten back to us by now, I tell Marci and Denis about the things Mom, Grandad, and I wrote down on the legal pad—the stuff to do *after* what we've already done, like write letters to the editor, protest, and contact the press, the publisher, and the American Library Association.

"Great list," she says. She seems far away. Her frown-dimple is still there.

"What's wrong?" Denis asks.

"I'm so tired of the patriarchy," Marci says.

Denis sighs. My shoulders get tense.

She adds, "This is clearly sexism at work."

The patriarchy is *a system of society or government in*

which men hold the power and women are largely excluded from it. Sexism is *prejudice or discrimination [typically] against women.*

"Please, Marci," Denis says.

I don't say anything or sigh. I try to hold my face in a smile but I can't tell if it's working. I really like Marci, but when she talks about women's rights, I feel bad because I'm a guy.

"That's the only reason this word is being censored. This specific word. Think about it," Marci says. "The world acts like boys are like computers that can't be reprogrammed to act sensibly, so they're 'protecting' you from a perfectly normal word. So dumb."

"Are there computers that can't be reprogrammed?" Denis asks.

Marci ignores him.

I can't think of anything to say.

"Don't you understand?" Marci continues. "You can't think feminism is just about girls. It's about you guys, too! The reason this book is censored is because people *expect* you to be immature and stupid. All boys. Sixth-grade boys. Too stupid to read about six million people who were murdered and not giggle at one word about a body part."

"You're right," I say. "It's sexism."

"It's disrespectful. As if you can't handle the word *breasts*!" Marci says.

"Breasts," I say. "I mean, if they're on a chicken we can talk about them all day, right?"

Marci looks at me funny for that, but I think it makes sense. Right then, Hannah Do walks toward us from the playground and waves. Marci and I wave back. Denis's back is toward her, so he turns around to look. He waves, too.

I say, "It's on the menu board at Wendy's. It says their tenders are made of one hundred percent chicken breast. Breast. It's right there!"

Aaron shows up. "Did someone say the magic word?"

We ignore him. Hannah Do stops walking toward us.

"Why are you ignoring me and talking about bad words over here?" Aaron asks.

"It's not a bad word," Marci says.

"Why are you so ignorant?" I ask back.

"Because it really makes people like you mad," he says.

"Go away, Aaron," Denis says.

I watch Hannah turn around and walk back toward a bench on the other side of the playground. It makes me mad.

Suddenly everything makes me mad.

My dad, the mug, the thing he said about not being able to love. Ugh. I'm mad that someone censored our books. I'm mad that Dr. McKenny acts like it's no big deal. But mostly, I'm mad that Hannah was too scared to come talk to us because people like Aaron like making people like me mad. And it worked because, fact: I am so mad.

Marci seems to sense something is wrong. Her eyebrows express a quiet concern. Then someone yells, "Watch out!" and Marci jumps up and catches a football that was headed toward a group of kids standing behind us. The whistle sounds, Marci hands the football to the recess teacher, who happens to be Ms. Sett, and we go back inside.

Three minutes into lit circle, the intercom on the wall clicks and the secretary asks for Marci to come to the office. Ms. Sett nods and tells her to go. Marci looks at me and Denis and shrugs. Ms. Sett has a smirk on her face, and I sense that she probably knows we talked to her boss about the censored books. I don't get why Denis and I weren't also called to the office. I get kinda mad about it.

Grandad told me a story once about what *divide and*

conquer means. It's a control method by people in charge to make the people *not* in charge fight with each other. I think that's what Ms. Sett and Dr. McKenny might be doing. If they divide me, Denis, and Marci, maybe we will stop caring so much about what they do wrong.

Either way, I worry about Marci too much to read the book. My brain just does that thing where it makes up scenarios about how Ms. Sett is going to punish us the whole school year, even though she's acting perfectly like herself.

Ten minutes later, Marci arrives back in the classroom with an oversized blue sweatshirt over her other clothes. I can tell she's been crying. I think she's still crying. She sits down at our group six pod of desks and picks up her book and pretends to read. All my anger from recess turns into concern.

"Are you okay?" I whisper.

"Shh. Read," she answers, but her lip can't even shush me all the way, it's quivering so much.

It's still hot in the school, and Marci's face looks red going on purple.

Ms. Sett comes around to each group and asks some quiet questions about what they're reading. When she gets to our table, she asks Marci, "Feeling better?"

Marci doesn't look at her.

Then Ms. Sett asks something about what Seder is and what Passover is and Hannah answers for us because Denis and I, and even Aaron James, are looking at Marci, trying to figure out what just happened.

When it's time for club block, Marci rushes off to chorus and I read ahead in the book, even though Ms. Sett has written on the whiteboard: DON'T READ AHEAD!

At dismissal time, Marci takes off the oversized sweatshirt, leaves it on her desk, and then almost runs down the steps. Denis and I have to jog to keep up with her, the whole time saying variations of "What's wrong? and "What happened?"

"She dress-coded me!" Marci explodes once we get outside.

"What's that mean?" I ask as we start walking home.

"Of course you wouldn't know," she huffs.

"It's not Mac's fault," Denis says. He turns to me. "It means that they made her wear that big sweatshirt because she was wearing something that was against dress code."

"You're wearing a T-shirt and—whatever those are called," I say. "What was—like—"

"They're called capri pants," she says. "And the

problem was, if I lift my arms up, like I did at recess, my T-shirt goes up."

Denis and I wait for more, but Marci just keeps looking ahead. I remember her catching the football at recess, but I don't remember what happened to her shirt when she jumped up and caught it. It all happened so fast.

"That's the dumbest thing I ever heard," I tell her. "If you hadn't caught that football, it would have hit a bunch of kids."

"Exactly," Marci says.

Denis is now walking with his arms up, and his T-shirt rises up about six inches. I can see the elastic part of his boxers peeking out of his board shorts.

I do it, too. My T-shirt goes up, and I can feel a breeze on my back.

"Don't rub it in!" Marci says.

"Sorry," I say. "I was just trying to figure out how long my shirt would have to be for it to not ride up like that."

"Halfway to your knees, I bet," Denis says.

"The patriarchy is so dumb!" Marci says.

We're quiet for a block, cross Main Street, and cross the road to be in the shade.

"How can it be the patriarchy if Ms. Sett is the one who dress-coded you?" Denis asks. I'm glad he does.

"The patriarchy is *everywhere*! It's a system! We live *inside* of it. Adults, kids." Marci points to the blob of younger kids walking ahead of us. "They all live inside of it, too. It never ends!"

"Does it say somewhere in the dress code that we can't lift our arms?" Denis asks.

Marci smiles a little. "Only girls, I guess."

"Volleyball is going to be difficult," I point out. "And basketball."

Marci smiles again. She doesn't say anything, but I think we made her feel better. But most of me knows that both Denis and I feel weird talking about the patriarchy and sexism because we're guys.

Right then, I realize why Mom has so much grace . . . and I feel bad knowing Marci is probably using grace right now to even talk to us.

She

———

The next day, Dr. McKenny gives all three of us an appointment during first block.

I never expected to be nervous, but Dr. McKenny smiles so wide when she walks in and closes the door behind her, it's creepy.

"I've done my snooping," she says, "and I know what happened with the books." She brings her hands together and holds them in front of her, clasped, making a point with each syllable. "So it's all over now. You guys can stop worrying."

Denis says, "We're not worried. We want uncensored books and we'd like to know why whoever did this did it."

"Well, it's obvious why she did it," Dr. McKenny says.

She. She said *she*. Marci looks at me and raises her eyebrows.

Then Marci tells Dr. McKenny, "It's not obvious to me." Marci's taking notes on a legal pad—Grandad would love her.

Dr. McKenny says, "The person who did this told me that while working through this book in earlier years, those areas of the book made some students very uncomfortable and made some of the boys in class giggle. Some of them complained, so she took care of the problem."

"I *knew* that was going to be the reason," Marci says.

"It's sad," Dr. McKenny says, "but true. Not all sixth graders are as mature as you three."

I'm skeptical. Adults do a thing when they lie to kids— they make up wild stories. She's doing that.

"The second passage says that she motions to her *undeveloped chest*," I say. "I don't understand how anyone could be uncomfortable with that. So I don't think anyone giggled. And I don't think anyone complained, either."

Dr. McKenny looks directly at me, and her smile is now two counties over. "Are you saying that I'm not telling you the truth?"

"I think I'm saying that I don't believe that anyone ever complained about this book. That's all." What I really mean is: Go ahead, tell me the last time a bunch of kids came to a teacher to tell her that they were made uncomfortable by a word in a book. This doesn't happen.

Denis adds, "Also, if this logic applies, I could complain to Ms. Sett today about the content of any other book and that means she'll censor all the copies in her room, right?"

"It *is* hard to believe," Marci says. "You have to admit that."

There is uncomfortable silence. A lot of it. Marci and I make eye contact and smile a little bit.

"I think we've said enough on this topic," Dr. McKenny says. "I'm glad you brought your concerns to me and we cleared it up."

"Are we going to get new books?" I ask.

"It's just a few words," Dr. McKenny says. "And you already know what they are!"

There is more uncomfortable silence.

"We didn't clear anything up," Marci points out. "You're still supporting censorship. So nothing has changed. Though now we've wasted a week. That's all."

"Thanks for your time, though," Denis says.

"Yeah," I say. "Thank you."

The three of us get up and leave her office as

Dr. McKenny looks at us with a mix of confusion and optimism on her face. Meaning: She's hoping she just stopped us but really has no idea if she did or not.

Fact: She not only didn't stop us, but she just made us more determined than ever.

The Day We Have Off
Because of Lies

None of us says anything as we climb the steps back to Ms. Sett's room. But when we get to the top of the steps, Denis says, "Guys, I'm scared that she's going to really be mean to us now."

"We can take it," I say.

Marci gives me a silly look. "We don't have to take it. We'll just complain if she targets us. I mean, we didn't do anything wrong."

Denis sighs. "We told on her."

"She's a grown-up," I say. "This isn't elementary school. I mean—well—you know what I mean."

"We have a lot to do now," Marci says. "I don't care if she's mean to us. I want new books. I'll do what it takes to get them." Denis and I nod and mutter different versions of agreement.

When we get back to class, Ms. Sett has the lights off and has a video cued on the whiteboard. "We have a day off school on Monday," Ms. Sett says. "Let's talk about why!"

She starts the video about Christopher Columbus. It's all the same stuff we learned in second grade. How he got here in 1492 and "discovered" America, how one of his three ships wrecked off the coast of Hispaniola, and how he was considered a hero in Spain. Nothing about how Columbus harmed the Indigenous population from the minute he landed. Nothing about how a person can't "discover" a place that was already there and populated by people who already knew about it.

I keep hoping that the video will say something more honest toward the end, but the narrator only closes with the rhyme we all learned when we were seven: *In 1492, Columbus sailed the ocean blue* . . .

The minute it's over, I put my hand up.

Ms. Sett says, "Mac?"

"I would like to talk about the truth about Christopher Columbus," I say.

She nods.

I continue, "He enslaved, tortured, and murdered

Native people and I don't think we should consider him a hero anymore. I don't think we should have done that in the first place."

"That's a valid opinion," Ms. Sett says. "But without Columbus, we wouldn't be here, right? And I don't know about you, but I like living here."

"That's colonization, not discovery," Marci points out. I'm glad she says it because I need time to gather my argument.

"I like living here," I say, "but I also know that if someone showed up tomorrow the way Columbus did, and took you and your friends and made you slaves, sold your young daughters, or killed a bunch of your family, you probably wouldn't be okay with it."

"He didn't make anyone slaves," Aaron scoffs.

Ms. Sett huffs through her nostrils and rolls her eyes. "This is really a discussion for high school. Or college."

"'The truth is a discussion for high school or college?" I ask, and as the words come out of my mouth, I realize I am not in full control of them. Something happened to me in the principal's office. I'm mad again. "Anyway, you said this classroom was like college on the first day of school. Why wait?"

"He didn't make anyone slaves," Aaron says again.

I turn to him. "Yes, Aaron, he did. First he took women and gave them to the sailors on his ships. Day one. Imagine he took your sister and gave her to strangers."

Hannah Do looks uncomfortable. I didn't want to be so blunt, but it's hard to suppress a superpower.

"Plus," I say, "he then enslaved the men in every place he found. He brought diseases that killed more than half the populations he came into contact with, and *then* when the slaves tried to revolt, he killed them and paraded their bodies through the streets. That was in the Dominican Republic, if you want to know. He was governor there."

The classroom is quiet.

Ms. Sett puts her hands together in a sarcastic soft clap and speaks slowly. "Again, Mac, I think this is a history lesson for when you're older. For now, let's just do our worksheets and get this lesson over with, okay?"

"So you want us to learn lies?" I ask. I am way too mad right now and I know I'm being disrespectful. I know better, but if she doesn't respect us enough to let us read regular words in a book, I don't see why I should respect her while she teaches lies.

"He didn't give women to sailors," Aaron says.

"Aaron, be quiet," Ms. Sett says. She looks suddenly awkward.

"You know," I say to her. "You know the truth but you don't want to teach it."

"We'll discuss it during recess," she says. "Here in my room."

I think I just got recess detention for telling the truth.

"Detention?" I ask.

She ignores me. "Let's get these worksheets done and we can move on to the geography of the Caribbean! I even have my own pictures from three different islands!"

I say it again. "Detention?"

She ignores me a second time.

"Open your computers and start on the two lessons in there. You have fifteen minutes."

I don't like being ignored. It's like pretending something isn't happening when it is. While the other kids do their schoolwork, I use the search engine to look up if there's a word for pretending something isn't happening when it is.

I make a bullet-pointed list of terms for it.

- Gloss over
- Sweep aside
- Kick something into the long grass
- Turn a blind eye
- Look the other way

My favorite is the one in the middle. So many things in my life this week have been kicked into the long grass, I feel like I live in the long grass. My skin gets itchy just thinking about it.

Recess detention is more long grass. Ms. Sett either forgets she gave it to me or she remembers and leaves me here by myself to think about why we shouldn't learn the truth about Columbus in sixth grade. Deep down I worry about how mad I am again, and I know the reason I got recess detention was because I couldn't control my mouth earlier and I wonder if that leads to smashing mugs.

Then, twenty minutes in, she comes through the door and sits down at my pod of tables. I look at her and have this hole where my respect used to be. I don't get how all my grace just disappeared today. But when I look at her, I can only see her sitting down and crossing out passages in books with a marker.

"I wish you wouldn't challenge me in front of everyone like that," she says. "I have a job to do and I must do it properly. Don't get me wrong—I know what Columbus did and I know what you're talking about. I just can't teach that stuff to kids this age."

"We're twelve," I say.

"That's young."

"It's six years from adulthood."

"True, but this is an elementary school. Your parents and the other parents of students in this class wouldn't appreciate that."

"Mine would," I argue.

This is when the bell chimes and we can hear kids in the hallways. Ms. Sett gets up and smiles and says, "I do understand that you come from a house that's different from the other kids'. But please try to just keep what you learn at home out of my lessons." The hole where my respect used to be gets bigger when she says *what you learn at home* in that tone.

"So the Earth can be flat?" I ask. This is kinda mean to bring up Aaron like this. I know it. I don't care. She just made it sound like my family is weird for talking about real things.

She looks at me like she doesn't get it and moves to her desk, sits down, and rummages through a pile of papers there, acting again like this isn't a big deal.

I explain, "I have to leave the truth at home, but Aaron James gets to say the Earth is flat in front of a geography teacher?"

She grimaces—like she's making a hard decision. I hope the decision is to stop teaching lies, but she also could have gas from her lunch.

"The class *knows* Earth is round," she finally says.

"But they *don't know* the truth about Columbus, which is why it's important to talk about it."

"They'll figure it out. Same as you guys figured out the words in *The Devil's Arithmetic*, right?" she says, leveling me with a look over her glasses.

I'm speechless as the room fills up with my classmates.

I look at Hannah, who's just sat down next to me.

I feel a little dizzy and not like myself.

"Are you okay?" she asks.

I say I'm fine, but really I'm mad again. Between the crazy rules around here, my dad being, well, my dad, and now this, I'm done hoping adults do the right thing. I'm done thinking they have our best interests at heart. Except for Mom and Grandad, I think they all live in the long grass, even if they know they shouldn't.

The Sickness

A few minutes later, my group sits around the lit circle table. I lean into Marci and Denis.

"She knows," I whisper. "She just said something to me about how we know what the words are in the book."

Both of them frown a little.

"Huh," Marci says. "Well, this probably isn't the first time she's censored books. She obviously doesn't care." Marci still has that little smile she had in the principal's office this morning. Grandad would say she has *spark*.

Denis says, "Why would she? She's always been Ms. Laura Samuel Sett, right? From the paper?"

"True," I say.

"We should talk to her," Marci says.

"Why?" Denis asks.

"Because maybe it's time to talk to the actual person who caused the problem?" she says. *Spark.*

Hannah says, "She'll be here after school today. I'm staying to make up a quiz." We all look at her like she just landed here, but she and Aaron have been listening this whole time.

Marci turns back to me and Denis and says, "We should talk to her today, then."

"Group six? Is there anything you need?" Ms. Sett asks from her desk.

We look over and say variations of "Sorry" and then look busy.

I pull out my book but I can't stop looking at Marci. Her hair is really shiny today.

"Dude, you okay?" Denis whispers.

I give him a thumbs-up and can't find any words. I seem to be filled with a feeling I can't talk about. It's like the opposite of mad. I didn't know it was possible to feel opposite things at the same time like this. It makes me feel like there's a tug-of-war in my stomach.

I ignore it and reread chapter five.

In chapter five, Hannah, the main character, continues to try to tell the people she has time-traveled to in Lublin,

Poland, that she is not from their place or time, but they continue to think she is a girl named Chaya. No one believes her or seems to care. It frustrates me the same as talking to Dr. McKenny this morning.

When Marci comes in from chorus practice later that afternoon, she looks happy about something bigger than usual.

Denis asks, "Why are you smiling?"

Marci shrugs and puts her notebooks into her backpack.

She probably likes some guy who's in chorus with her. I can't sing in tune and I don't really listen to music and Marci is in love with every pop song and oldies and even punk rock, which she says is the language of people who fight oppression.

We all get our backpacks together and get ready for the walker dismissal announcement. When it comes, the other students leave and we go to Ms. Sett's desk and stand there until she looks up.

"Hello, three musketeers," she says.

"We wanted to talk to you about the book," I say.

Denis adds, "We didn't want to get you in trouble."

"We just wanted to get new books and raise awareness about censorship," Marci says.

Ms. Sett laughs a little under her breath. "I don't mind at all," she says. "You'll learn, as you grow up, that adults in your life seem to be doing things you *think* are wrong, but really we're helping you."

"Wait," I say.

Marci says, "Censoring books isn't helpful. For anyone."

"Yeah," Denis adds nervously.

"No one is keeping you from reading the book," Ms. Sett says. "You're reading the book."

I think Marci might explode at that, but instead she remains calm and says, "You censored it. Which means you made a decision about what we can and can't read. It's unconstitutional."

Ms. Sett lets out a genuine laugh. "Oh, Marci, you need to have more fun in your life. Same goes for you," she says, motioning to me with her head. "And in terms of constitutionality, I think you'll find the Supreme Court has given schools some leeway about what goes on in the classroom."

"With all due respect, we don't plan on stopping our fight," Marci says.

"With all due respect, I wish you luck," Ms. Sett says. She has a look on her face like she's enjoying this. I can't explain it. It's not passive-aggressive or manipulative—two definitions I learned from Grandad when Dad first moved out—but she's, like, sure she's right.

Hannah is waiting over by the door to take her quiz and two other kids are here, too. The three of us walk out of the room, giving Hannah high fives to her raised palm. I think we're all holding our breath because, once we get out of the building, we all exhale big-time.

"Wow," Marci says.

I shake my head. "She really thinks this is all fine."

"Maybe we should just let it go," Denis suggests. "I mean, she's the teacher and we can't win, right?"

"If you want to stop, you can," I answer. "But I'm here to fight this until we get at least a little respect."

"Exactly," Marci agrees. I swear when she says this, my heart skips. I can't look at her because I start to feel my cheeks going red. "I'll see you guys tomorrow."

Marci walks in the direction of her house and I stand there watching her for a second or two, forgetting Denis is standing right next to me.

As Denis and I walk home, we play a bunch of rounds of BOT DUCK MAN. He wins, I think.

I don't know. I'm not paying attention.

"You good?" Denis asks.

"Yeah," I say.

Silence takes us over for more than a minute. I'm about to tell Denis that the thing in his bug bite from last summer is really an unhatched cat, but then Denis asks, "You like Marci, don't you?"

"Yeah," I say.

"I think she likes you, too," he says.

"It's so dumb. We should be— Wait. You think so?"

"You should go to the homecoming dance together," Denis says, then smiles and peels off toward his house.

When I get home, I head right for Grandad's flat.

Grandad is sitting on his floor cross-legged (he calls it *lotus*) and holding his string of beads. He tells me to join him, so I sit the way he's sitting.

"Did she lay into you about Columbus?" he asks.

I nod and roll my eyes.

"You okay?" he asks.

I sort through my thoughts and feelings. 1. I am okay. 2. I had a heck of a day when it comes to my teacher finding out that we tattled on her, and 3. she still thinks she's doing the right thing when she lies to us whether through videos about the Columbus myth or with a Sharpie marker.

4. I felt a lot of anger today and I don't even know if that makes me okay or not okay. 5. But right now I feel like I'm going to throw up and that seems to be the most important thing.

"I think I like a girl," I say. "But I really don't because I can't actually like this girl."

Grandad looks serious. "Do your hands sweat?"

"Yes."

"Do you get all swampy around her?"

"Swampy?" I ask.

"You know, everything's damp?"

"I guess."

"When you think about her, what does it feel like inside?"

I think about it. "Like I'm scared."

"Oh boy," Grandad says. "Can you eat around her?"

"Not as much as usual."

"Does she like you back?" he asks.

"Denis says she does, but I don't think so. I mean, she's smart and in chorus and she plays the saxophone and she's always talking and reading and—"

"Don't sell yourself short, Mac. You're a smart guy and you have lots of cool hobbies."

"I don't have any hobbies," I sulk.

Grandad thinks about it for a second. "You help your dad in the garage on Saturdays. And you eat candy with me!"

"And I help my mom make awesome soup, yeah," I say. "I know. None of those things are mine."

"Well, what do you like to do?"

I think about it for a few seconds. "I like to be bold and change the world and stuff. Like I want to write a real history book that doesn't lie and buy an electric car and I want to go to protests when I'm older because things need to change and my friend Marci should have the same rights as men do."

Grandad looks at me a long time. "Ah . . . so it's Marci?"

I nod.

"Let's figure out what to protest," Grandad says.

"Yeah."

"I already know," he says. "Don't you?"

I look at him. He should know my brain isn't working. I'm sick with whatever this is. "I could protest the homecoming dance because . . . uh . . . homecoming is stupid?"

"Ya think?" he asks. "I always thought homecoming was cool. Didn't know you had a dance at your age, though."

"That's what's stupid," I say. "I mean, it's a lot of pressure on kids our age."

"I suppose, but it doesn't seem protest-worthy," Grandad says.

"Huh. Okay. Well, I don't know what to protest, then."

Grandad gives me a serious look. "I'm not going to tell you. That's just wrong." When I'm still quiet, he says, "It's what you've been thinking about all week."

"Oh!" I say. I mean, duh.

"Looks like you have a hobby," he says. "In the meantime, let's get you some records. I think you need to listen to more records."

"Okay," I agree.

Grandad takes three deep breaths with his eyes closed and rolls the beads on his string between his finger and thumb, stopping at the last one, and then does this praying-hands sort of thing with the beads wrapped around his hand. Once on his forehead, once on his mouth, and once on his heart. Then we get up and walk to the music store.

I find three punk rock albums. He buys them for me and throws in a love song compilation from the 1970s even though I tell him not to.

"You gotta learn about love somehow, kid," he says.

Longest Day Ever

By the time Grandad and I leave the record store, it's nearly four o'clock. Grandad has to go to a weekly meeting at his veterans' club until five and Mom doesn't get home from work until 5:30. So when I get home, I go to the kitchen for a snack and sit down on the couch with my school computer.

I check my email. No reply from Jane Yolen yet.

I check my grades. All good.

I check the school calendar and see that the homecoming dance is three weeks away.

I'm about to search for how to ask a girl to the homecoming dance, but then Dad walks in the front door and it's Thursday, so it feels like an emergency.

"What are *you* doing here?" I ask.

"Uhh—aren't you happy to see me?" he asks back.

"Sure," I say, "but it's Thursday and—does Mom know you're coming over tonight?"

"Yeah. I'm staying for dinner." He sits down on the other couch and puts his feet on the coffee table.

"Oh. Okay. I have some stuff I have to do upstairs," I say. "I'll be down in a little bit." I pick up my computer and take it to my room. I don't know why. I just don't feel right being alone with Dad in Mom's house. Plus, Mom would have told me if he was coming today. She always reminds me.

I sit on my bed and open my laptop and barely have time to type in *How to ask a girl to a dance* when I hear Dad walking around outside my room. I hear him open the linen closet door and close it again. I hear him move toward Mom's room. Something about it makes me get up and go to the hallway.

"Oh! Hey there!" he says. His hand is still on the doorknob to Mom's bedroom.

"Why aren't you in the garage?" I ask.

"Do I always have to be in the garage?"

"Well," I say, "yeah. Kinda. I don't think Mom wants you up here. Not in her room, anyway."

"I was just checking things out. Bus dropped me early."

I know and he knows that the bus didn't drop him off

early—he just caught an early bus. He lies with the same ease as Denis gets freaked out by snakes.

I know the only way out of this is a diversion, so I say, "Let's go play catch."

He turns around and starts back downstairs, which I take for a yes. But then, on our way down the steps, he says, "I can't really play catch, though. My arm is hurting today." His arm seems fine to me. But I don't tell him that. Instead I say, "Okay. Let's just sit outside or something. Mom should be home soon."

We go out to the porch and sit on the patio furniture. He looks around and doesn't say anything. Finally, Grandad comes home and saves me. If Grandad is surprised to see Dad, he doesn't show it. I need to work on that.

"Mac," Grandad says, "you need to empty the dishwasher. I'll keep Mike company."

I say, "Okay," and go inside and find the dishwasher already emptied. When I look back out to the porch, I can see Grandad leaning forward and talking to Dad with a serious look on his face.

I don't think Mom knew he was coming.

I don't think Mom wants him here on a Thursday.

I don't think he was invited to dinner.

I don't know what to do with my own dad. He thinks

he's not from this galaxy. And he's acting more and more like that every day.

This has been the longest day of my life. It's like I lived a week from the eight a.m. meeting with Dr. McKenny until recess detention. And another week between then and now.

Mom finally comes home close to six and is balancing two pizzas from our local pizza shop. (She'd have gotten it delivered, but they passed an ordinance last year banning pizza delivery in the town borough.) I take them from her and put them on the table and get busy finding paper plates and getting glasses out for drinks. The fact that there are two pizzas makes me understand Grandad already texted her to let her know Dad is here.

"You're such a good kid," Mom says. She smiles at me, then walks over and kisses me on my head. She takes a deep breath of my hair and I don't get why she does that, but when I asked last time, she said it's because I still smell like I did when I was a baby. Weird.

At dinner I tell Mom, Dad, and Grandad about our second meeting with Dr. McKenny, how we know it's Ms. Sett, and how she said that kids had complained. I explain what Marci said about how this is all about the patriarchy and how we need feminism because it's good for everyone.

"Oh wow!" Grandad says. "She's a firecracker!"

I smile. "Yeah," I answer. "And at the end of the day, we talked to Ms. Sett, just to make sure she knew we aren't trying to be mean or anything. We just want to not have censored books."

"What'd she say?" Mom asks.

"She acted like crossing out words in books is a totally normal thing to do. Just like the principal did."

Dad says, "What did they censor?"

"The word *breasts* and another vague mention of a girl's chest," I say.

Grandad asks, "So your next stop?"

"Superintendent. And a school board meeting, probably," I say.

"I still think you should write a letter to the author," Mom says.

I don't tell her I already did. It's as if the reality of Dad smashing Mom's blue mug is in that letter because when I think of the letter, I think of the mug. So I haven't told anyone I wrote it because just like my dad smashing things, it's now a secret I want to keep.

She adds, "And don't forget I'm coming to talk to Dr. McKenny tomorrow. Maybe I can get this moving faster."

Grandad nods.

Dad doesn't say anything. He just eats pizza.

Aliens Don't Like Feminism

"Let's roll!" Dad whispers. I heard him come in, but I thought I was dreaming.

It's past midnight and I'm exhausted but I say yes because, well, I'm not sure why. I can't sleep. I have too much on my mind. Deep down I think he might be able to help me with Marci. He's my dad, right? He might have something more helpful than records full of love songs.

I put on a fall coat over my sweatshirt and we roll the craft out of the garage as usual. He gets the engine going so we can fly. Right now, we look a lot like two guys in a vintage car. Gravity is still in play.

"I think I might finally have this thing fixed," he says once we're on Main Street.

"Cool," I say.

"You're twelve, so that means it took me thirteen years."

"Yeah."

"So how do you think it would be if we took this baby for a real ride?" he asks. "All the way out?"

"I need to go to school tomorrow."

"Of course," he says, but without really agreeing. He sounds like he's never been my father, or anyone's father for that matter.

I try to find the courage to ask him about what it feels like to have a crush or to ask him how to have a girlfriend. If anyone would know how weird this feels, it would be someone who thinks he's an alien.

"We don't have to go back right away," I say. "But soon."

"Good," he answers. "Because we have to talk."

"Oh."

He sighs. "This whole thing you were talking about over dinner—this feminism thing. It's a way to bring us down as men."

"Whoa. Wait," I say. "Anyone who thinks censoring a book because boys need to be sheltered is dumb."

He hits the gas suddenly and I'm frightened. At first, we pass a few cars on the wrong side of the road.

"I don't like being called dumb," Dad says.

"Then you should be with me on this censorship thing. The whole reason it happened was the teacher underestimates boys and sees us as dumb."

"I see it as her protecting you," Dad says. "And protecting girls. I'd be embarrassed to be a girl with boys reading that word in the same room as me."

"Why?"

He says, "Think about it. Imagine if a boy-parts word was there instead."

I just heard my father say *boy-parts word* instead of using an actual word. For parts we both have. I don't know what to do with this.

"Let's try testicles," I say.

"Hey!"

"So if the word *testicles* was in the book, in a scene where Nazis are surrounding young boys naked in the shower and yelling things at them, would we cross it out so girls wouldn't giggle?" I ask.

"We would cross it out because that's harmful to boys!"

"Using the word for their own body parts?"

"Why is it even in a book for kids anyway?"

"Because kids have body parts and words for those parts are normal?" I answer. "And in this case, to show a very realistic scene in a concentration camp."

"I can't talk about this anymore," he says. "We're going to have to agree to disagree."

That's what Mom always says to him. I'm not really sure if she means it, either. It's her way of kicking him into the long grass, I think.

"Deal?" he asks.

"Whatever," I say. "I'm cold. Can we go home?"

I feel him look at me and I keep looking forward.

"I didn't mean to make you mad," he says.

"Not mad," I tell him.

"What are you, then?"

"Figure it out, alien anthropologist."

"That sounds mad," he says.

I sit for a moment and try to figure out what I'm feeling. Not like it's a huge surprise to find out that my dad thinks feminism is dumb and that we can't talk about body parts like normal people. But it's . . . something.

"Disappointed," I say. "That's what I feel."

"Oh."

I keep looking forward.

By the time we get home, Dad has tried four space jokes and a funny jingle. I keep looking out the windshield and don't laugh once.

LGBTQ+ Kids Need Our Help

I watched a girl get bullied on her walk home from school yesterday. Kids walked behind her yelling gay slurs. I told them to stop it as they walked by my porch, but they laughed at me. It's time this town woke up in the twenty-first century. These kids need our help, not to be bullied, hidden, or canceled. Show your support by flying a Pride (rainbow) flag if your family is LGBTQ+ friendly! —Jane Jones, Front Street

Re: LGBTQ+ Kids Need Our Help

I'm sure I'm not the only one in this beautiful town who wants to keep the bedroom out of our schools. Please, try the Bible club in the high school—see what they have to say about your rainbow ideas.

—Laura Samuel Sett

I am the president of the Bible Studies club at the high school and I just want to say that God loves everybody—no exceptions. Also, we fully support the school's Gender and Sexuality Alliance and some of us belong to it. —Brittany Hummel, Walnut Street

Recess Inside My Head

I t's recess, it's still too hot, Marci and Denis are in the shade of the doorway, and I take a walk on the macadam loop around the playground because I'm so tired I will fall asleep if I sit down.

"Heads up!" someone yells, and I look up and duck just in time to miss a football that seems like it was purposely thrown at my head. It lands a few feet away and bounces oblong until it stops on the grass.

Aaron comes to get it. "Sorry, dude," he says.

"No problem. Thanks for the warning."

"You were daydreaming. Probably thinking about animal rights or something, eh?" he says.

I don't tell him that my dad kept me up way too late last night and also can't say words for his own body parts.

"Your boyfriend is looking for you," he says, and points to Denis, who is walking toward me past the playground equipment that feels too small for most of us now.

"Grow up for once," I say.

"Sure, sure. Gay rights or whatever," Aaron says, then runs off with his football.

It almost makes me feel good—to know that I will never be like Aaron James.

"Hey!" Denis says. "Marci wrote the letter to the school board to request a spot at the meeting and she wants you to read it."

"Now?"

"It's just a letter," Denis says.

"Fine."

"You okay?" he asks.

"Sure. No. I'm fine. Just daydreaming," I say. We walk toward Marci, who has a pencil in one hand, a piece of paper in the other, and the look of concentration on her face. Her dimple is out and it's still cute. Ugh.

"What are you daydreaming about?" Denis asks.

I shrug. "I keep thinking about *The Devil's Arithmetic*," I say. "I read chapter ten last night and the train boxcar scenes are really sad."

"But—" Denis says, "we're on chapter six. No reading ahead."

I hold my hand out. "I don't follow rules, remember?"

We sit in the shelter of the school door entrance and read Marci's letter. "I like it," I say when I'm done. "My mom is coming to talk to Dr. McKenny after school."

"I was really hoping to do this ourselves," Marci says. "But I think we'll need help."

"I can't stop her anyway. It's her tax money and she already made the appointment."

"I think it's okay if our parents try," Denis says. "I mean, if they can get somewhere we can't, then that's good, right?"

"Hey, that reminds me—would you guys be interested in protesting on Main Street tomorrow?" I ask. I can't make eye contact with Marci.

"Protesting what?" Denis asks.

"This whole thing," I say.

"Wow," Marci says. "That's cool."

I shrug like it's no big deal. "My grandad and I are going to go up and just sit in front of Tad's with signs for a few hours and talk to people starting at ten. It can't hurt."

"We're going hiking tomorrow," Denis says.

"I can go! I'll make signs!" Marci says. She's smiling, and that makes me smile.

"Heads up!" someone yells.

This time, Aaron's football lands inside the small vestibule, bounces off the walls, and hits Marci in the face. She checks her nose for blood and brushes off the spot that was hit the hardest. A redness forms around it.

The recess teacher blows her whistle and kids start lining up to go back to class. I help Marci to her feet and say, "You okay?"

"Yeah," she answers. "Am I bleeding?"

"No. You look great," I say.

Denis has already walked up to the teacher and we can see him explaining it to her. She looks at Marci and frowns. She finds Aaron and stands next to him as we walk inside.

Aaron isn't in class for the first ten minutes of lit circle.

He misses a vital change in our group.

Hannah Do says she has something to tell us. She says, "I know you've called me Hannah since I got here in first grade, but my real name is Hoa and I want you to call me Hoa from now on."

We all nod and she adds, "The character in this book— *she's* Hannah. I'm not Hannah. And the way she changes names—because she time-traveled to this horrible time in history—made me see that I shouldn't use that name anymore."

"Why did you change your name in the first place?" Denis asks.

"To make English-speaking people more comfortable. *Hoa Do* is considered 'too Asian,' so a lot of us just adopt English names to get through easier, you know?"

"That's not cool," I say. I sound like Grandad.

"It's not," she says. "But even in Asian countries, they tell Asian people to adopt an English name. It can make it a lot easier. Trust me."

"I love the name Hoa," Marci says. "I think it's beautiful."

"Me too," Denis says.

"Me too," I say.

Hoa nods, and we go back to the lit circle question Ms. Sett gave us to do today. *Do you like the book? What are your favorite parts?*

So far, all of us are liking *The Devil's Arithmetic.* We discuss the time-travel element of the book and how it's a cool way to tell this story. We talk about how the girls in 1941 can't believe that Hannah has toilets inside her house. It's hard to pick a "favorite part" of a novel that's about something so awful. But those comparisons—we agree those are our favorites so far.

Hoa asks, "So are we going to do anything more about the crossed-out parts? We're getting close to them and I want a new book."

"We're working on it," Marci says.

"If you need any help, tell me," Hoa says. "My dad is a lawyer, and he would be so mad if he knew about this."

"You haven't told him?" I ask.

"He'd probably schedule a meeting with the principal first thing in the morning if I did."

"My mom is coming in today," I say. Marci still looks a little pained about it, but I don't mind. It's nice to see that an adult around here cares about something as important as this.

At that moment, Aaron walks in, sits down, and says, "What did I miss?"

Not one of us tells him about Hoa. Not even Hoa.

Later on, while I wait for Mom in the school office, I daydream about protesting with Marci and I get kinda nervous about it. I calm myself with the fact that Grandad will be there and he can make small talk with anyone, anytime.

"Mac?" Mom says.

She's standing there and Dr. McKenny is there and I must have spaced out and daydreamed a bit too much.

"We're all done," Mom says.

"Oh," I say. "I think I fell asleep or something." Dad really shouldn't be taking me out on school nights.

Mom turns back to Dr. McKenny and says, "Just remember, Peggy. This is not what schools do."

"It's just a few words. They're still reading, right?" Dr. McKenny replies.

Mom shakes her head with grace and thanks the principal for her time. When we get out of the office and into the parking lot, she curses in a string. "She thinks I'm dense," she says. "Like this is funny or something."

"Yeah," I say.

"Like I'm some kind of kid!"

Oof. Sometimes, it's like adults can't hear what they say when they say it.

Still Processing

As we drive home, Mom tells me what happened in the meeting and then doesn't say much else because she says she's still processing. I guess I am, too. When Dr. McKenny said that thing about how we're still reading the book, she missed the point. I'm sad she keeps missing the point. She's a principal. She should know how to not miss the point.

But more than that, she should know how to treat my mom. Mom is a tryer. She gives people a lot of chances to do what they say they'll do and she trusts people—even when she probably shouldn't.

"How do you feel about it?" Mom asks.

I'm mad, but I'm somehow pretending I'm not. It's like I've inherited long-grass disease from the grown-ups around me. "I don't know," I answer. "I think she should care more."

We park and get out of the car. I get the mail from the mailbox because it's my favorite thing even though no one ever sends me anything. There's a magazine and two bills for Mom.

We walk into the house and see the same things at the same time. We both freeze two steps into the living room. Some of our stuff is gone. It looks like we got robbed by a burglar who does interior design. Mom's favorite chair is still here, and the rocking chair, too, but the rug that was under them is gone. The dining table is here but the center-piece is missing.

The bookshelves are gap-toothed—random books seem to be gone.

The rug from in front of the kitchen sink—gone.

"Dad?" Mom says. She knocks on his basement apart-ment door. Opens it. Repeats, "Dad?" Grandad doesn't answer. It's Friday. He's not usually gone on a Friday.

She fast-walks around the house and I follow, finding weird empty spaces where our things once were. One of a set of table lamps. A small pottery vase.

"My knitting bag?" she says.

"My baseball stuff isn't in the closet," I point out.

She jogs up the stairs to her bedroom. I go to the garage door and open it.

The spacecraft is gone.

His tools are gone.

"Dad?" I yell.

Mom is upstairs yelling, "Mike?"

I yell, "Grandad?"

She yells, "Dad?"

I go upstairs to my room. Nothing seems to be missing. It's the same mess I left it as this morning on my way to school. For some reason at this moment, I make a deal with myself to clean up my room every night so Mom doesn't have to say anything to me about it.

"Dad?" she says.

I go to her room. She's on her phone, sitting on her bed. All the family pictures she'd framed and put on the walls and the furniture are still there but two paintings are gone, the screws that held them still in the walls.

"Where are you?" she asks him.

All Dad's dress clothes are gone from the closet where he kept them. It's like we were robbed but also abandoned at the same time. I'm not stupid. I know what's happening. I just didn't think Dad was this mean. Or whatever this is.

"I think Mike cleared out the house and took off," she says. And in that last part, I can hear her voice buckle under itself. She stays still on the bed. Sighs. I hear Grandad say, "I'll be right there."

Mom hangs up the phone and looks at me. I look at her.

Then she offers me a hug and all the mad I was hiding in the car is like a tiny little fish and this huge other fish just ate it and absorbed the mad and now I'm like a huge mad fish that wants to eat all the little mad fish so I can become a fish capable of eating a whole planet. A galaxy. Dad's galaxy. I want to eat that.

"I am so sorry," Mom says as we hug.

"You didn't do anything wrong," I tell her.

"I don't even know what to say."

I can feel her tears seeping through my shirt. I think there's snot running from my nose and I don't care.

"You think he just left? Like—forever?" I ask.

"I don't know," she says. "I just don't know."

"I'm so mad. I don't understand."

"Why would he take our things? Those were our things!"

"He took my baseball stuff," I say. "He doesn't even like baseball."

"Oh, Mac, I'm so sorry. We can replace it. I promise."

I don't tell her about the lucky rock in my baseball backpack—the one from the game when I hit my first home run. I don't want to make her feel worse.

We sit like this for a few minutes—hugging and saying things that seem unreal. Asking each other questions we can't answer. *Why did he take a vase? Why did he take the rug?*

Before Grandad gets home five minutes later, we breathe a lot and really look around. Dad took some light bulbs and batteries from the light-bulb-and-battery drawer. "And my face cream," Mom says. "Why would he need my face cream?"

I thought I'd seen Grandad mad before. After he hugs Mom and gives me a hair ruffle at the same time, and after he looks into my mom's eyes real close-up and says, "We will get through this," he holds his arms out and breathes a huge breath and then he walks to the garage door and sees how empty the garage is and lets loose a deep howl and curses about ten bad words over and over and over. He walks around the empty space in the garage and then sits down cross-legged on the cement floor and closes his eyes.

I go to the kitchen and get a glass of water for Mom, who is sitting in her chair, now with no rug under it. She thanks me and says, "Get one for yourself, too, bud."

The garage door is still open and Grandad is still sitting and meditating on the floor.

I get him a glass of water and one for myself, and by the time I'm out in the living room again, Grandad is there and he looks calm.

He says, "I'm calling the police."

The Truth

Grandad and Mom let me stay up until midnight. We put on punk rock music and move the furniture around after the police leave. Mom and Grandad take pictures first, of every inch of the house the way it looked when we got home, like the officer suggested, and we start a list of all the missing stuff. By midnight, the list is two pages long. We even leave off the weird stuff. A paper clip holder. Fragrant soap. Toenail clippers.

We move the living room around so it faces the dining table—Grandad says, "That way we can't ever have our backs turned to each other." Mom orders a new rug on the internet and reorganizes her books.

I sit in the spot on the cement floor where Grandad sat earlier in the day and I try to meditate the way he does.

All I can do is picture Dad flying through space with my baseball stuff poking out the back window.

Mom and Grandad talk pretty loud sometimes. Mom cries a little, but Grandad keeps saying she's "better off" and then they talk about the mug.

"He knew what he was doing," Grandad tells her.

"I know," Mom says.

"He was never gonna change, kiddo," Grandad says. "He was just getting meaner."

"I know," Mom says.

In the morning, as I sit at the dining table munching on a bowl of cereal, I look around and the place feels new. Even with all our old stuff, something about it feels completely refreshed and comfortable.

But when I see Mom at first, she looks like she cried all night. That's not new at all.

"How you doing?" she asks.

"Good."

She gives me a hug and kisses me on the head. "I love you like crazy, Mac."

"Love you, too," I say.

"It's all very sudden," she says. "You're probably in shock."

I nod and chew. Cheerios are so delicious.

She starts making herself a cup of tea and Grandad arrives from the basement. "I slept until seven thirty!" he says.

Mom laughs.

He says, "First time in months I managed past five." He looks around. "The place looks great."

"I'm not in shock," I say.

"I didn't say you were," Grandad says.

Mom goes quiet while she pours water into her cup, then says, "I did, Dad. Sorry, Mac. I shouldn't tell you how you're feeling."

And now I feel bad because I don't want Mom to be apologizing to me. Not today. Not ever. I might be in shock. But I'm not as in-shock as she is because I know the truth and she doesn't.

"I have something I have to talk to you about," I say.

Mom sits in her usual seat at the table—across from me longways—and she feels too far away for me to talk about this. It feels like it should be whispered. Without Grandad here.

Neither of them says anything.

I look at Grandad and he raises his eyebrows and says, "I'll be back in ten minutes. Nature calls."

I rinse my cereal bowl and leave it in the sink and sit down closer to Mom.

"Look," I say. "This is going to sound really weird, but just listen, okay?"

"Okay," she says.

I breathe big. Twice. Then: "Dad kept something from you for a long time and he shared it with me and it always felt wrong that I knew this and you didn't."

She looks worried.

I continue, "He doesn't think he's from Earth. He thinks he's not human. And the secret we worked on in the garage was his spacecraft."

The moment hovers. She looks me right in the eye. "Spacecraft," she says.

"He used to take me for rides in it late at night when you and Grandad were sleeping. Not a lot. Like once a month or so. Usually to eat junk food," I say. "He'd say he was from two galaxies away and is kind of like an anthropologist, here to learn about us and live a normal human life to be able to report back. It's probably why he took such weird things when he left."

Another moment hovers. "Anthropologist," Mom says.

"I know it sounds like he was just making up a story for me. And sometimes it seemed like it was just a story. But other times, it was like he . . . meant it. He wanted to fix Grandad's old car so he could get home. He said he'd been stuck here for—"

"Thirteen years?" Mom interrupts.

"Yeah."

She sits with this information for a minute and nods and purses her lips. She goes to say a few things but stops herself until she finally says, "You'd go on, like, flights? In space?"

"Not space, really. He couldn't break the Kármán line," I say. "That's sixty-two miles above Earth's surface. We probably only got up to a mile, maybe. He kept saying he needed elements we didn't have here. He told me he was probably stuck here for life."

"I know the feeling," Mom says.

She seems to be taking this too well. "So you knew?" I ask.

"I knew he was stuck. I didn't know he was an alien. We'll keep talking about it."

"Does Grandad know?" I ask.

"We should tell him," she says. Then she sends him a text on her phone and he arrives so quickly, I know nature did not call and he was probably waiting on the steps until we were done.

"I'm hungry," he says. "Anyone want pancakes?"

The Truth II

Grandad laughs when I tell him what Dad said, just like I thought he would. He's making the best pancakes you'd ever eat. Adding blueberries to his and chocolate chips to mine. He says, "I'm amused, Mac. I've waited my whole life to meet an alien and all this time . . ."

"Dad," my mom warns.

"I knew he was weird. I mean, I even told you that time he ate peanut butter with his tortilla chips. That's *got* to be an alien thing."

Mom is smiling now, and it's kinda funny. I think I'm smiling, too.

Grandad says, "Between that and the way he never wiped his shoes off."

"And he couldn't really sneeze," Mom says. "For

real—not even if he got dust or pepper up his nose."

"And he never played catch or did anything I wanted to do," I say.

I really thought they'd approve of my contribution, but instead, I stop the conversation cold.

I say, "What? He didn't. He was only interested in his ship. That's where he'd spend time with me, but he wouldn't talk to me or anything, besides asking me to hand him a wrench or whatever."

Mom says, "I'm sorry, Mac."

"For what?" I say. "You play catch with me all the time."

Mom and Grandad look at each other in that way that adults do. Mom chews the inside of her cheek like she does when she's thinking hard about taxes or how to solve a problem.

Grandad says, "I'm sorry, guys. I meant that to be sarcastic. Or funny or something. I guess I make light of things that cause pain. Old habit."

"Mac," Mom says. "You have to switch gears for me. I know this will be a bit hard. But, um . . ."

"I knew you would do this," I say. "Adults always want to say that weird stuff isn't weird, but—"

Grandad interrupts me. "I think plenty of stuff is weird, son, but here's what I think—your dad isn't an alien; he's just kind of a jerk. And that wasn't a spaceship. It was my car." He takes a deep breath.

"Sometimes our brains make reasons and stories for other people to help them make sense to us." Mom says this so softly, I can't even get mad at her. "If he was pulling you out of bed in the middle of the night, while Grandad and I were asleep . . . I can't imagine what stories he'd tell you when you were half-awake."

Grandad says, "With the top down, that car can feel like a spaceship, I guess."

"It wasn't just a car," I say. "Not to him."

"That's true. It was a very special car. Your gram and I—uh—well, we did things in that car that were—uh—full of love," Grandad says.

"That's not what I meant," I say.

Mom and Grandad stare at me and I just know they're going to say something about how I should go talk to my mom's sister, Aunt Diane, who's a counselor.

The two of them are looking at me like I'm a rescue kitten in a shelter window. Mom even has tears in her eyes.

"Mac," she says. "Come here."

She gives me a really nice hug and her tears end up in my eyes and it's weird how she did that. "I'm so sorry, buddy," she says. "It really is a car. I've been in it many times. It was our car when I was growing up."

"The Karmann Ghia," I say.

"Yep," Mom says.

Grandad grunts a little, like he's remembering the car and all the memories in it. It's a mix of "huh" and "hmph" and "mm."

I don't understand myself right now. I don't know what to say. Because I guess there was always a part of me that went along with everything Dad said, to the point that I could even have memories of flying in space with him. I don't know how I can have memories of something that didn't happen. Like—twenty times. I know the difference between the anime I make up in my head and reality. I mean, I think I do. Right?

"Maybe he was really an alien or magic or something and he could make me believe the car could fly," I say. "Because I really believed I flew in that car."

"He was magic all right," Mom says.

"Yep," Grandad says. He finally sits down to eat after serving me and Mom. He doesn't use maple syrup—never has. He says that the fruit is sweet enough. This is the town candy freak.

Maybe he's the alien.

Maybe we're all aliens.

Bona Fide Human

Marci Thompson is not an alien. I've never met a more annoyingly determined and punctual human being in my life.

It's Mom who answers the door.

"Hi, Ms. Delaney," Marci says. "Is Mac here?"

When she gets to the kitchen, the table is still covered with syrupy plates and forks and crumbs, empty mugs and half a glass of orange juice that I couldn't stomach after the syrup and chocolate chips.

"Good morning, Marci," I say before she even rounds the corner of the hallway. I hear myself say it. I sound forty and like Marci is coming to my office. As if last night I was a sixth-grade boy and this morning I'm some kind of insurance salesman.

"So. Are we ready to go?" Marci asks.

Grandad says he has to get his bucket of candy. I put my shoes on. Marci hands me a sign. It says STOP CENSORSHIP AT INES!

"Do you have anything more snazzy?" I ask.

She holds up her sign. INTELLECTUAL FREEDOM IS A RIGHT.

"We're going to have to work on some slogans," I say.

"Yeah. I can't say it was my most inspiring sign-making night. My cat kept throwing up."

Grandad arrives with his bucket and a baseball hat so his head doesn't get sunburned. He grabs three lawn chairs and we say goodbye to Mom. I don't want to leave her today. Sometimes I think I don't want to leave her ever.

"Are you sure you don't want to come with us?" I ask.

"I have errands to run. Don't worry. I'll keep myself busy."

I wish I could tell you that the protest is exciting, but it's just me and Grandad and Marci sitting outside Tad's with our signs and eating candy. It isn't much different from any other Saturday when we eat candy. The same old people stop by to talk to Grandad. They ask me and Marci questions just to be nice.

"What's going on with those signs?"

"They're really censoring books?"

"Do you think you can stop them?"

A few tourists stop and ask what the signs mean. Marci shows them the black rectangles in her book. One guy offers to give a donation but Grandad says we don't have a need for money. Just for action.

The whole time, I think about how I'm treating what Dad did like he's a guy who works in my office who resigned and is getting a job somewhere else. Not a big deal. Whatever. But on the inside, I know I'm not okay. I'm mad for how he hurt Mom. I'm mad about my baseball stuff. I'm mad he lied to me and made me look like a dumb kid because I believed him. Each thing that makes me mad, I put it in a dull-colored folder and file it in a gray filing cabinet.

We protest for three hours, have a lot of cool conversations with people, and then Marci says she has to get home. Grandad says we should get some lunch, so we start walking home, too, with Marci at first until she takes a left to go up her street.

"See you on Monday, Mac," she says. She opens her arms and I think she's going for a high five, but then she hugs me and I hug her back kinda—my right arm is still raised for the high five that never came.

Grandad and I walk quietly after that. When we get home, we go to his flat to put the candy bucket away.

"That was fun," Grandad says.

I don't know what to say at first, but then all these feelings hit me at once and I say, "I feel like I work in an office."

He looks confused.

"I feel old. Like I'm in an office and I'm handling all this stuff like a real office guy," I say. "Not like I know what it's like to be an office guy but you get what I'm saying, right?"

"You are one cool cat," Grandad says.

"None of it feels cool."

"I mean you have a way with words, kid. When you write a letter to that author, you should ask if she can help you write a book. I bet you could."

I tilt my head and wonder if Grandad is not hearing me on purpose or if he's doing it by accident. It makes my eyes wet and I take a deep breath, but when I exhale, the quiver from my lip moves to my chest and it comes out like I'm shivering. Or crying—which is what I seem to be doing.

But like an office guy, I don't feel like I'm crying, I'm just crying—same as asking people to come into my office and leave work on my desk or empty my trash can like that's normal. I don't feel a thing. But I also feel my whole body shaking and it's like it's not my body. I'm twelve, by the way.

This is when Grandad wraps his arms around me.

My whole body goes limp the minute it knows he will support it. I am a sobbing blob of 100 percent human. I never wanted to be half alien. I never wanted any of this. I just took it in and filed it. Dad told me he was an alien, and I believed him because he's my dad. I saw the McDonald's parking lot from a half mile high. I did all that. I made my own anime series about us in my head and wrote and drew every episode and every season.

Feels like it was for nothing.

Not just because he left and stole Grandad's car and my baseball stuff, either.

When he said he smashed Mom's mug last week—it felt like it was for nothing every time he got like that. And he got like that a lot. It's hard to know when they're sitting right there at your dinner table with you, but people can be real jerks while you make up excuses for them.

"You just get it all out," Grandad says, and I do—for what feels like ten minutes.

When I finally sit up and gather my used tissues from

the floor, and Grandad stretches his right arm and shoulder, I say, "Sorry for crying."

"Don't you dare be sorry for crying," Grandad says. "Crying is one of the most important things to learn how to do."

I laugh. "Nobody has to learn how to cry," I say. "Babies do it!"

"Next up, talking. Babies do that, too," he says.

"Hey! I talk," I say. "I even get in trouble in school for talking!"

"You're great at standing up for the abolition of Columbus Day, but most days you keep your feelings inside. You get what I'm laying down?"

"Yeah," I say. "I get it."

For the rest of the night, I still feel like an office guy, though.

Unreasonable Curfew

My son and his friend were driven home in a police car last weekend because the officer said they were out past curfew. I was not aware of this 9 p.m. curfew and I don't understand how we are enforcing it. My child and his friend were simply taking a walk and did nothing wrong. Plus, some restaurants on Main Street are open until 11 p.m.! Do the people leaving them and walking to their cars also get ticketed for such ridiculous things?

—Mike Fallon, Locust Street

Re: Unreasonable Curfew

Those who stay up to all hours are known to have lifestyles that bring a town like this down. Good people are asleep or close to it by 9 p.m. and two boys walking and talking outside others' homes can wake up people who have to work in the morning. Try to think of others and keep yourselves and your children inside after 9 p.m.!

—Laura Samuel Sett

The Crush

O n Sunday we go canoeing. We never go canoeing. This is what families do when something big and weird happens. They do things they never did before. So we go canoeing. It's still warm, but not hot. The lake is big and motors aren't allowed, so it's quiet. We see herons and egrets and a turtle sunning itself on a log.

Mom has to work on Monday, but I have the day off because of the big lie. So Grandad and I sit around, play backgammon, and watch a movie that tells the truth. It's called *Blackfish* and it's about orcas in captivity and what their lives are really like, and it's really sad. After that, we put on the punk rock records he bought me and he tries to teach me how to dance punk rock.

"Here's the thing: There is no specific way to dance to this stuff," he tells me.

"Usually they just throw themselves around the mash pit or whatever it's called," I say.

"Mosh, I think."

"I just like doing this." I stand and tap my foot and bang my head to the beat.

"You do you," he says, and then thrashes himself around his flat like he has helicopter blades for arms.

At dinner, we talk about the Lenape tribe, and we recognize and thank them before we eat. People do that in a lot of countries that took land from Indigenous populations and Mom does it before every event at her work. It's called Indigenous Land Acknowledgment and today seems the perfect day to start doing it at our house.

Tuesday is normal. It's still hotter than it should be and I think it's affecting us. In math class, I can't remember anything we learned last week.

After lunch, we have library class. We've been learning how to research and I'm still trying to find any articles about books being censored like ours are. I hear Denis and Marci talking in the shelves behind me, so I get up from the computer station and stand closer.

"Mac totally likes you," Denis says. My heart drops into my shoes and I feel a sudden need to run while my body stays completely still.

"He does?" Marci asks.

"A lot." I don't know how to feel—other than like an office guy.

"Huh. I thought he thought I was bossy," Marci says.

"You *are* bossy," Denis answers.

There's silence that scares me a little and the two of them start laughing.

"Huh," she says.

"Why not go to the homecoming dance with him and figure out if you like him?" Denis offers.

Marci laughs through her nose. "Oh, I like him. I've liked him since fourth grade. Did he send you to tell me this? Why isn't he telling me himself?"

"He doesn't even know I'm telling you," Denis says. Part of me wants to be angry when Denis says this, but honestly, I'm glad he's telling her. Now I don't have to.

"Oh."

"He can't stop talking about you and I'm getting sick of it," Denis says. A complete lie. I don't ever talk about Marci. "And if you go to this dance with him, then he might stop or the two of you can kiss or whatever and it will just get all of that weird stuff over with."

"You make it sound like it's not normal."

"I don't want to kiss anyone ever, and that's just how I am," Denis says.

"Ever?" Marci asks.

"I've never even had a crush," Denis says.

"Huh," Marci says.

"What?"

"What if you knew that I liked you once?" Marci says. "Does that make you like me back?"

"No," Denis says. "Sorry. I really love you as a friend, though. I think you're really smart and great!"

I can hear the crack in Denis's voice and I know I should rescue him. I slowly walk up the side passage between rows of books. I act like I'm really thinking about something deep, and then I look up and see the two of them there and say, "Oh, hey. I was just looking for you."

"Hi, Mac," Marci says.

"Hey, Marci," I say. I smile.

"Is it true that Denis has never had a crush?" Marci asks. Denis looks at me and smiles crooked.

"It's true," I say.

"Huh," she says.

"More crush energy for the rest of us." I smile at Marci. Marci smiles back.

I feel like I'm going to puke up all my lunch.

When I get home, Grandad is in the yard meditating again. I don't want to interrupt him, so I turn back and head inside, when he says, "Don't go! Come. Join me."

"I really can't," I say.

"I'm not asking you to do anything but sit down," he says.

I walk to him and sit down.

"Doesn't the grass feel good in your toes?" he asks.

I still have my shoes on. I take them off. I'm self-conscious because I know people say boys' feet smell, but I take my socks off, too, and put my toes in the grass.

"You're tense," he says.

"I guess I always am."

"Nah. You're a chill guy. Your gram always said you were a little lamb." His eyes are closed and he's smiling as he says this. He looks so at peace. Breathes in. Breathes out. "You're just in a choppy ocean at the moment."

The grass is making my toes itch. Things just feel wrong here on the tiny lawn with the neighbors watching. They probably think Grandad is a weirdo for sitting here breathing and humming all the time, rubbing magic beads.

"Good day at school?" he asks.

"Yeah. Just normal."

"Any news on the school board meeting?"

"As far as I know, they're going to let us talk. Marci said she got approval," I say. "Now we have to find ways to get more people to help us."

"We'll keep protesting on Saturdays," he says.

"Yeah, I have to go. I have homework."

This is a lie. I feel bad lying to Grandad but I'm still processing the fact that Marci has liked me since fourth grade.

Chapter Eleven

The thing about *The Devil's Arithmetic* is that up until chapter eleven, the reader, like Hannah (the main character), is experiencing the journey of Jewish people from their villages and home places in train boxcars—eventually landing them at concentration camps.

Until chapter eleven, the story is about the journey—and I know where they're going because I know what the Holocaust is. And so does the main character because she's a time traveler. But the people in the story don't know—just like in real life. It's eerie and you can tell something terrible is about to happen, but at first, it's just . . . normal.

Jane Yolen sure knows how to write a book.

Today is the day we read chapter eleven. Of course I've already read it, and so have Marci and Denis and Hoa. Aaron is the only one in our group who probably hasn't.

I pull out my uncensored copy of the book and start reading.

The horrible shower scene unfolds and Aaron doesn't say anything about his censored book until he sees my page because I put my book, open, flat on the table. Yes, on purpose. Of course on purpose.

"Hey," Aaron says. "How come my book has that part blacked out?"

"What?" I say.

"Let me see." He reaches over and grabs the book. I grab it back. He asks, "What page is that?"

"Ninety-three," I answer. I put the book down again, with my hand on it to keep it open.

"Someone crossed out a bunch of words on my copy," he says.

"Mine too," Marci says.

"Same," Denis adds.

Hoa nods.

"How come you got a copy without it?" Aaron asks me.

"I bought this one myself."

"Huh. Why?"

"Because if they're censoring books, what else are they going to hide from me, right? What lies can they be telling me, you know?"

Aaron nods and squints at me. "Are you messing with me?"

Marci and Denis show their censored books.

"Well, what's it say?"

Marci smiles at me, then turns to Aaron. "You're not going to believe it," she says. "But Ms. Sett censored it because she thought boys—like you guys—would be uncomfortable and get all weird about it."

"Imagine," I say, "uncomfortable during *that* scene! As if it's not already so terrifying."

"But what's it say?" Aaron asks.

"It says *hands over her breasts*," Hoa says in a quiet, respectful voice.

Aaron frowns. No giggles in sight. He looks at me and I give him my book so he can read it. He gives the book back to me. "That's just *wrong*."

"We *know*," Marci says.

"What can we do about it?" Denis says. "We have to do what they tell us, right? I mean, rules are rules."

I give him a look like we're going too far.

We sit quietly for a few moments. Hoa goes back to reading her book. Marci does, too. Denis follows and I go to pick up my book. Aaron says, "Where'd you get that copy?"

"Tad's."

"Was it expensive?"

"Four bucks used. They have new ones for eight," I say, then go back to reading like censorship is no big deal. Aaron mutters under his breath a few times about it. He's still frowning.

"You okay, Aaron?" I ask.

"I just don't like people telling me what to do. It's a free country, right? This is covered in the constitution, I bet."

"First amendment," Marci says. "It's kinda the most important thing."

"Huh," Aaron says.

Hoa says, "If you ask me, the word made the person who crossed it out more uncomfortable than it makes us."

"And she even has breasts!" I say.

As if she can sense our topic of conversation, Ms. Sett turns our way and says, "Mac? Marci? Why is there talking and not reading?"

"Sorry," I say.

She gets up and approaches us.

She pulls a spare chair from another pod and sits on it. "What chapter are you on? Last I checked your worksheets, Hannah and the family were still on the train," she says.

"We just got to chapter eleven," I say.

"The showers," Marci says.

"Oh," Ms. Sett says. "That's a tough scene. Today's worksheet has a space on it to talk about how it makes you feel. Make sure to really write your feelings down there."

What occurs to me right then is that my feelings about this scene are horror, sadness, and shock, but because she made the scene about her own censorship rather than the content of the book, I feel distant because I was more curious about the black rectangle than I was paying attention to the book. It makes me even more determined to fight the whole thing.

"I feel angry," Aaron says, "that someone thought they could censor my copy of the book. Like I'm too dumb to read the words that are meant to be here." He looks super angry, too.

Ms. Sett says as she stands, "Just write it down on the worksheet!"

"Huh," Aaron says.

"Is there an issue, Mr. James?" Ms. Sett asks, hand on her hip.

"Actually, yeah, there is," Aaron says. "I think this is un-American and wrong. I think my right to read the words here are covered by the first amendment or another part of the constitution. And I think this is tyranny. Like—don't tread on me, okay?"

"I'm sure no one was trying to tread on you," Ms. Sett says.

"Yeah, well, whoever did this is going to have to hear from my dad. He's real into freedom and so am I."

Ms. Sett walks to her desk and sits down behind it and barely hides the smirk on her face. She still thinks this is nothing.

I hope it works. It had better work.

Ice Cream

We meet at Greco's after school on Friday because Marci said we would. Greco's is one of the reasons I love living in this town.

"I can walk out of my house, and ten minutes later I can get anything I want," I say.

"Except milk and bread," Marci says. "Which is why this town needs a little grocery store."

"You and your grocery store!" Denis says.

Marci shrugs. She's been talking about the lack of a small grocery store forever.

"It's practical," I say. "It's the one thing we're missing for a basic, normal, walkable town."

"Exactly," Marci says. "The whole point is to not have a car. Save the planet. All that stuff."

"Yeah," I say.

"Are you two going to run it together?" Denis jokes.

I try not to smile, but the thought of running anything with Marci makes me smile because she's so organized and I'd be happy to do whatever she wants. Ugh. That sounds so bad. But it's not like that.

When we get to Greco's, we take a minute to look at the menu board. They make their own ice cream and they have everything—milkshakes and soft serve and sundaes and Italian ice—thirty flavors easy. But we're here for the homemade and I choose a small regular cone of butter pecan. Denis gets chocolate chunk and Marci gets a waffle cone with a scoop of chocolate and two scoops of butter brickle.

We sit outside at a picnic table, and even though it's October, it still feels like summer.

"I wonder what Aaron told his dad," Denis says. For the past few days of lit circle, Aaron has been turning every page, waiting for more black rectangles to appear.

Marci says, "We shouldn't be focused on Aaron. We should be focused on the school board meeting."

"I've been writing notes," I report. "I still can't find any real research about this kind of censorship. There's a lot of banned books and book challenges. I mean *a lot*. But this blacking-out doesn't seem to be officially reported. I don't think it's because it's rare. I think it's probably common. I can't tell."

"They sure make it seem common," Denis says.

"Our main focus is trying to get a policy in place," Marci says. "The one thing we've read everywhere is that when books are banned by one or two decision-makers, the goal is to set policy in place so it can't happen again without a larger group of people making the decision."

"Hold on," Denis says. "I thought we were trying to get new books."

"Look," Marci says. "People won't take us seriously if we just ask for what we want. The whole reason we're protesting is for us, yes, and getting new books, yes, but it's really so the kids who come after us don't have this happen to them, too."

"I'm sure if our copies are censored, other books in her classroom are, too," I say. "So policy would be great."

"Exactly," she says. "Plus, my parents are all about policy. They say they could write it in their sleep. So for Tuesday's meeting, I'll have a sample of the policy we want them to use."

"My dad works for the phone company and my mom programs computers. I don't think they know anything about this kind of stuff," Denis says.

They look at me. I nearly tell them that my dad thinks he's an anthropologist from another galaxy . . . until I remember that he doesn't really think that. Until I remember that I haven't told them anything about my dad and how I can't seem to find the right time or the right words.

"Are you coming to protest with us tomorrow?" I ask Denis.

"Yep. I even have a sign."

"Excellent," Marci says. "I was thinking of handing out flyers about what's going on, but my dad told me to wait until after the meeting. We can hit them hard with the facts then, and spread the word after. He says that's fair."

"Seems fair," I say.

We start walking toward the street and Denis peels off to go to his house. When it's just me and Marci, I almost ask her to go to homecoming with me, but I don't.

There are way too many files on this office guy's desk for today.

Not Fun

The three hours on Main Street on Saturday morning are not fun. Grandad can see it. He keeps saying stuff like "You have really great friends!" and "Boy, I wish I had a crew like this when I was your age."

Denis brought a sign that says CENSORSHIP IS WRONG.

Marci has her signs from last week and I prop the extra one up against the back of my chair, but don't hold any. I'm used to holding wrenches and car parts on Saturdays, not signs. It's not like I loved that stuff, either, and it's not like I want to see the guy, but he's my dad and I guess I'm getting used to it.

By noon, when Grandad goes to the food truck to buy us all hot dogs, Marci and Denis have noticed I am in a mood and are no longer trying to get me to smile or be part of the conversation. It feels like the wrong time to tell them the truth about what's going on.

By the time we pack up our chairs and leave, Marci and Denis are playing BOT DUCK MAN and it makes me furious. I don't say anything, but I can feel myself frowning. And I can see them seeing me frowning, but they don't stop playing. It feels like they don't want me as a friend anymore.

Once it's just me and Grandad walking back to our house, he says, "What's going on, Mac? You don't seem like yourself."

"I'm myself."

"Okay," he says.

We keep walking.

He says, "Denis told me that there's a dance coming and you want to go with Marci but haven't asked her yet."

I think really hard on this before I say anything. Fact: I'm not even sure I want to go to the dance with Marci.

"Mac?"

"I don't know," I say. Maybe I just need to live in a cave by myself for the rest of my life or something.

"I think you're having a hard day," Grandad says. "We should probably take it easy and play games or something."

"I'd play catch but my glove is gone," I say.

"Ah," he says—in that way like this sentence solves bigger mysteries.

"What?"

"Let's go get you a new glove and bat and everything. Your mom said that was on her list for this week, so I'm sure she'd be thrilled if we did it for her."

"But what if Dad comes back and brings my old ones with him?" I ask.

He nods and says, "Well, if that happens, we can always donate the new stuff to someone who needs it, right?"

An hour later, I'm trying on baseball gloves and they smell like new leather and it makes me miss my old glove. But I'm happy when we walk out of the store with a new bag, bat, and glove, with a batting glove and a big bag of Swedish Fish thrown in for fun.

As we drive home, Grandad says, "So are you scared to ask her out? I mean, at your age, I couldn't do that stuff, either. So maybe you could write her a letter. You're good with words, you know."

"I don't know," I say. "I'm not scared. I can't figure it out. I think I don't trust her or something. I don't trust anyone."

"Oh. That's not a good place to be," he says. "Do you trust me?"

"Of course," I answer.

"Why do you think you don't trust anyone? You were always the kind of kid who gave people a chance."

I know the answer to the question. I'm not a psychologist, but I totally know this has something to do with why there's a new baseball glove on my lap and my mood all day. Dad. Dad leaving. Dad being so impossible to understand.

"You're right," I say. "I always give people a chance. I'm probably just having a bad day."

"Dinner will help," he says.

He turns up a song on the radio for the last five minutes of the drive home. I think about how the last week has been foggy—I'm here but I'm not. I feel like I have a secret because I kinda do have a secret. Not being able to be my true and honest self around Marci and Denis has been painful, even though it's kinda always been that way thanks to my dad being, well, who he is. Being fake is like lying and I hate lying.

They probably didn't mean to hurt my feelings with BOT DUCK MAN, but it's not like they know what's going on because I haven't told them yet. Everything is moving so fast. Plus, if I really want Marci to come to the dance with me, I have to ask her. But every time I think of it, I feel like I'm lying if I don't tell her about my dad. And

I don't feel like talking about my dad. Because I don't know what to say about my dad.

I go to bed early after oiling my new baseball glove and wrapping it up in a rubber band, the way Grandad taught me to when I got my old glove. The whole time, I still feel like an office guy in my office, sorting through filing cabinets, looking for an answer.

I don't even know what the question is.

White (House Paint) Only

When did the rule about house paint come into effect? I went to the paint store yesterday and talked to them about what colors I'd like to paint my house and they told me I can only paint it white due to my address and a recent ordinance. Who thought this was a good idea? And how can we change it?

—John Zimmerman, Main Street

Re: White (House Paint) Only

Everyone knows that white is the best color for a house. Especially in a town with so much history. Back when the founders came here, the only way to paint a house was with lime whitewash and all homes were white. To maintain the look of history, going back to all white is a great idea. I applaud all who have followed the rules!

—Laura Samuel Sett

The School Board

On Monday and Tuesday at school, Denis and Marci treat me like they always did—like I'm their best friend. It makes me feel guilty because I feel like I'm lying to them. I almost told Denis about my new glove, but then I didn't because he'd ask me what happened to my old one.

I keep trying to find a good time to tell them about what happened, but it never appears. Plus, Marci is so stressed out about the board meeting, I don't want her to think about anything else. She's our spokesperson and she needs to be sharp, as Grandad would say.

So I play the part of an enthusiastic team player, and Denis and I help Marci go through her main points over and over again, until finally, the Tuesday-night meeting arrives.

■

We have to wait almost until the end of the board meeting to speak. By this time, Denis has a nervous-leg-bouncing reaction and is vibrating the whole room. There's a lady in the row in front of us who keeps asking him to stop with her eyes like she's our mom or something.

I'm glad he's jiggling his leg so much because it's keeping my mind off how much my hands are sweating.

"We're ready to hear from you," a woman in a pink shirt finally says.

Marci walks a censored copy of the book to the place where the board president can take it from her. She then does the presentation she practiced on me and Denis perfectly. Denis and I stand behind her and nod and I am not prepared when a man on the school board says, "Mac, how do you feel about it?"

The man is a guy Grandad talks to on Main Street when we eat candy.

"I think it's wrong in a few ways," I say.

He motions like he wants me to continue.

"First, censoring anything is wrong. Second, censoring this particular material, in a book about the Holocaust, is wrong, and last, the reasoning behind it—at least what we were told—suggests that boys and men are in need of sheltering and if not sheltered, might be uncontrollably inappropriate. Which is sexist and wrong."

The room is suddenly quiet and all I can hear is the blood rushing through my ears.

"Where are you reading this book?" another board member asks. I see Marci's mouth move. I know she is answering. Still can't hear anything except for my blood.

I have this entire imaginary scene play out in my head where all the men in the room lecture me about how I shouldn't have any interest in sexism and how I will have a miserable life if I listen to what women have to say and one guy says, "You need a father around your house to show you the way," and then I think of Dad and how he showed me the way, all right, and I look back at Marci and she's looking right at me and I'm still thinking about—

"What?" I ask.

"What do *you* think a good solution would be, Mac?" Marci says.

"Oh. Easy. Tad's books can replace all the ruined books with new copies."

Denis adds, "We need a policy for the district so this doesn't happen again when just one person thinks something is right for everyone."

The crowd grumbles. I can't tell if they agree or not.

Marci says, "Here's a sample of policy for challenged books for you to consider when drawing up your own." She hands out eleven copies of her proposed policy. It's a lot of big language but basically it says that if anyone in the school district wants to censor or remove a book from anywhere, they must bring that book or content to the school board, who will decide the matter with the superintendent and a panel of teachers and community members.

"You know, I think this word might make girls uncomfortable, too," the board member holding the censored copy of the book says.

"Breasts?" Marci says. "But girls and women have actual breasts."

The room goes quiet for what feels like an unreasonable amount of time. As if Marci has just cursed. I feel a rising need to speak up.

"There isn't a person in this room who wouldn't cover their breasts or other private parts if they were twelve and naked with Nazi concentration camp guards yelling at them," I say. "You should read the book." I want to add more. My throat closes.

More silence. The board looks over the policy sample Marci handed them.

"Is there anything else we can tell you?" Marci asks. "Before you make your decision?"

"I think this is enough," says the man sitting next to the woman in the pink shirt.

"It's time for old business . . . starting with the bleacher situation," another guy says.

Marci half raises her hand. The three of us are still standing here like we're at a piano recital or something. "Um, so that's it?" she says.

"You can sit down. Come to the next meeting."

"But we need the new books now," Marci says. "By next meeting, we'll be done reading. Can't you pass this part now and then adopt the policy later?"

"I'm sorry we can't move any faster," the guy says.

"But this is a special case, right? It's happening now! You can stop it!" I say.

"We can't move any faster," the guy repeats.

I've decided all adults are liars. Except Mom and Grandad.

"We'll discuss it," the woman in the pink shirt says.

"It's not that hard," Marci says. "I don't see why you can't make a decision now."

She seems so broken by what's happening. Her feet are glued to the spot on the floor where she's standing. I put my hand on the top of her shoulder to help her come back to reality and go sit down with us.

She turns and follows, but when Denis and I sit down again, she just keeps walking.

Right out the door. Right down through the parking lot. She doesn't even wait for her parents to drive her home.

She walks so fast, we can't catch up until we get to the park.

"Are you crying?" Denis says.

"Of course I'm crying," Marci tells him.

"Don't cry," I say.

She turns to me. "Crying is a natural reaction to disappointment. Would you tell me not to sneeze?"

Funny, but in order to make this logical argument, Marci seems to have stopped crying.

"I should have practiced more. I don't even know if what I said made sense," I say.

"Why are you so hard on yourself, dude?" Denis asks.

I shrug.

No one says anything. I hear Denis's question

bouncing around in my head. I don't know the answer, but I am 100 percent convinced that it's my fault that the board didn't give us an immediate answer. They all looked so—judgmental. Like they knew my dad left and they knew he stole my grandfather's car and my mom's rug and my baseball stuff.

I guess that answers Denis's question, then.

"This is how boards work," Marci says. "They have to take the time to think about what we talked about and they have to gather facts and stuff."

"Exactly," Denis says.

"Then they make a decision about what to do," Marci says. "It's going to be a month at least, unless they decide it's a special case."

"I think it's a special case," I say.

"You made that clear," Marci says. She isn't making eye contact.

Denis points to the sky. "Look! It's Jupiter!"

"Are you mad at me?" I ask Marci.

She sighs. My whole body feels like it's turning inside out.

"No, I just hate waiting," she says. "And I'm still mad. About the whole thing. They treat us like kids."

I think all three of us think that's a funny thing to

say because we all smirk a little after a few moments.

"That's the thing," Denis says. "I'm tired of being treated like a kid but I also really like not having to make dinner or do laundry."

Marci smiles. Looks at me. Stops smiling.

"Are you sure you're not mad at me?" I ask after about half a block because that's all I could wait. Denis trails behind us because he's looking up at Jupiter.

"Oh, I'm sure," she says.

"Why are you so serious when you look at me?"

"Serious?" She smiles.

"Yeah."

"Mac, if you can't figure it out, I'm not going to tell you."

"That hardly feels fair," I say.

"Nothing today has been fair, I guess," she says, and then splits off down Cherry Lane, and I keep walking and looking at her walking away until I walk into a tree branch that nearly breaks my head open.

Telling Denis

After Marci leaves, Denis and I walk down to Locust Street.

"So you like Marci—so what? Why are you being so weird lately?" he asks.

I shrug and can't find words. Again. Dad took my words with him, too—while leaving little shards of Mom's mug all over my life. I feel like I'm living inside a giant black rectangle.

I'm quiet for a bit and then I finally say, "My dad left town two weekends ago. He stole a bunch of stuff from the house, including my grandfather's car, and just took off. We don't know where he is."

Denis stops walking. Looks at me. Sees I'm serious.

"That's awful. I'm so sorry," he says.

"Yeah."

"You must be really mad. Or sad. Are you okay?"

"I don't know. I think so?"

"Is your mom okay?"

I answer, "Thankfully, we have Grandad. He helps us both."

"But still, that's your dad. Like—has he called or anything?"

"No."

Denis puts his hand on my shoulder—the one nearest to him. We walk for a while like that and I feel better. I think of a bunch of things to say but can't figure out which one to say, so I don't say anything.

When we get to where he needs to turn right, Denis squeezes my shoulder and says, "You sure you're okay?"

"I'm good," I say.

My voice cracks and I hope he doesn't hear it. I'm doing all I can to keep the cracks on the inside.

"Okay," he says. "See you tomorrow." He takes the right and walks down Main Street. I keep going straight down Locust. By the time I pass the intersection where my house is, I'm crying and trying not to cry, which makes me cry worse.

I can't go home.

So I walk to the park. It's dark, which is the best time to cry.

There are three teenagers under the pavilion, so I walk across the bridge and then down the bank of the creek and then under the bridge, and I sit there on the big rock, head in my hands, and cry about everything. The board meeting, Marci, Dad, Mom, Grandad, Gram. I cry about all of it. I think about Hannah in the book— *The Devil's Arithmetic*—and I cry for her and for all those people who lived through something so impossible to understand. I cry because the world is a cruel place. I cry because sometimes things don't make sense. I cry because I feel bad for crying. I have a nice house, a nice mom, a warm bed.

By the time I get home, there's no way to hide the crying from my face.

As it turns out, nobody notices. I watch the end of a show Mom and Grandad are watching and then go to bed.

The rest of the week crawls by, class by class, math problem by math problem. Every day I feel farther away from Marci and Denis. They're so normal and happy. They still play BOT DUCK MAN together and I still feel jealous. But then on Friday, at recess, Marci comes up to me and says, "Hey—I can't make it to the protest this weekend. I have to help my mom do some stuff in the garden. And . . . Denis told me about what happened with your dad and I'm really sorry it happened."

Everything in my body wants to be nice and say thank you and all that stuff, but instead, I look around until I find Denis and I fast-walk over to him.

"You told her?" I say.

He doesn't say anything.

"You're my best friend! Why would you tell her something I told you in secret?"

"I—uh—I just thought—" he sputters.

Marci is here now, standing behind me. "He thought we might be able to help," she says.

I look at Denis. "You could have at least asked me first!" I look at Marci and then back at Denis. "There's nothing you can do to help. I can't even help myself. I don't even know why I told you." Then I walk right to the teacher on duty and ask if I can go to the nurse.

When I get to the nurse's office, she asks what's going on and I tell her I have to go home.

"I can't just send you home," she says.

"I have to go home. Just call my grandad. He'll understand."

So she does. Grandad tells her to have me wait and

he'll be here in a few minutes. After he picks me up, we drive in complete silence. He doesn't even ask me what happened. When we get home, I go straight to my room, which still smells like baseball glove oil, and I take a nap.

I miss dinner. When I get to the kitchen to eat something, Mom has gone to a yoga class and Grandad gets my plate from the fridge and reheats it for me. I get a glass of water. I feel like crying the whole time and it really bugs me. Even in all the years my dad only came on Saturdays, I didn't feel like crying this much. I feel like someone put a time bomb in my office filing cabinet. It's just ticking.

The weather got a little cooler—I need a jacket after dinner to go sit with Grandad in the grass, which he says I have to do, so I do it. He tells me that he's going to a protest in the city tomorrow—something about teaching real history in America.

"Sounds fun," I say.

"You can come along if you want," he says. "It's right up your alley."

I don't have anything else to do, so it seems like a good idea.

The City

Saturday comes, and so does the local paper. The letters to the editor cover a full page. A quarter of them are about us.

Censorship Is Wrong

Our rights as Americans are being silently taken from us by strangers. Our children's right to read books is a fundamental right and I applaud the kids who came to the school board meeting Tuesday night to fight for the rights of our children. We should support them!

—Nettie Mase, Elm Street

Re: Censorship Is Wrong

When I was young, children listened to their elders. They knew we knew what was good for them. It's a shame to see kids run loose like this. Their parents clearly have no idea how to raise them.

—Anonymous on Broad Street

That one stings. It makes me think of Dad, because he really didn't have any clue how to raise me. And it makes me think of Mom, who has enough to worry about without letter writers putting her down.

"Mac? You coming?" Grandad asks. "You and me, taking over the world, kid."

I put the paper down, put on my sneakers, and walk to the bus stop with him. Something in me wants to hold his hand, which I know I can't do. Right when I think that, he puts his arm around my shoulder and says, "You're heavy today."

Grandad still talks like it's the 1960s. *Heavy* means *serious*.

"Yeah."

"Heavy is a good way to protest," he says.

"Sure."

"It's the only way things get done around here."

We play twenty questions on the bus and arrive in the city. Grandad knows the way to the square where the protest is, and I can hear a crowd of people and someone speaking through a microphone. *Our kids are our future!* I see two teenagers walking in our direction. They both have signs. One says TEACH TRUTH and the other says STOP LYING TO CHILDREN.

"I didn't bring a sign," I say.

"Next time, you will. No big deal."

"What's the point if I don't have a sign?"

He looks at me and I can tell he's done with me being heavy. I'm even done with being heavy myself but I don't have any other option. I guess some days, or weeks in my case, are just heavy.

We get to the square and the crowd is big. Bigger than I expected. A woman is talking about how young people should learn the truth in school and how Columbus Day is an insult to all of us. Grandad gets a premade sign from a woman who's handing them out. Actually, he gets two, but when he hands me one, I say no, so he holds a sign up in each hand.

I am too heavy to handle this. The crowd is making me feel like I can't breathe. There are too many people.

Too many strangers. Too many voices talking. Too many thoughts in my head. *I don't belong here.*

The woman talks for another five minutes, and I listen and look around and read other signs to keep myself distracted. IF YOU'RE COMFORTABLE LEARNING HISTORY, IT'S THE WRONG HISTORY. CENSORSHIP CAUSES BLINDNESS. FIRST THEY BURN BOOKS; THEN THEY BURN BODIES. The clouds drop rain on us and some people have umbrellas and some start to leave. I turn to Grandad and he's clapping, signs under his arm, and smiling and he puts his fist in the air.

"I want to go," I say.

"We just got here," he answers.

But he sees the look on my face. He puts his arm around me and we walk away from the square.

A block later, he asks, "Did the crowd get to you? Too big? Too loud?"

I nod. We keep walking. The rain falls harder and we're both soaked.

"I don't get it," I say. "Why am I scared of everything now? I thought getting older would make me less scared."

Grandad nods.

I keep talking. "I don't want to be this scared going into middle school. The other kids will know and they'll pick on me."

"Back up, Mac," Grandad says. "I need you to understand something important."

"I'll get beat up and stuff," I tell him.

"Hear me out on this."

We keep walking. Grandad points to a bus shelter that's empty. We go sit in it.

We don't sit side by side like usual. He straddles the bench and looks right at me, so I do the same.

"Mac, you're going to be scared of a lot of things in your life," he says. "It's a crazy feeling, being afraid, isn't it?"

"Okay," I say.

"Listen to me. Are you listening?"

"Yeah."

"Okay," he says. "I need you to hear to this."

I nod.

"When I got shipped to Vietnam, I didn't know what to expect. I was only six years older than you are right now. And I was full of fear." He clears his throat. "I was afraid of my dad because he was strict. I was afraid of my boss at the restaurant where I worked because he was always making me feel small. I was afraid of girls—all of them. I was afraid of everything. I'd just graduated high school and I was afraid of the future. You know?"

"That's how I feel," I say. "Like—I'm twelve and I don't know anything about anything, so I'm scared of all of it."

"It gets a little worse," he says. "I don't want to scare you, but fear is something that gets worse before it gets better. Anyway, the thing is, well—I don't know what I'm trying to say."

"I'm scared that school is just a series of lies and people just keep repeating them and then we all have to live inside a big world of lies and I can't live like that, Grandad."

"That's why we fight the lies," he says. He gestures to his protest sign.

I get the urge to cry again. I wish it would go away.

"I see you," Grandad says, "holding back tears." He waits a few moments and adds, "Can I ask you a question?"

"Sure."

"What are you so ashamed of?"

I didn't expect this question, this bus shelter, or this feeling of wanting to throw up. If I threw up now, I think it would be all salt water. I suddenly feel like I swallowed the ocean.

"I can't talk about that here," I say. "We're in public."

"Public? No one can hear us. We're alone in a bus shelter."

"Shame is private," I say.

"Only if you let it wreck your whole life, it's private," he says. "Which is what most people do. I aim to bring you into the light, Mac Delaney. Shame is no way to live. And you have nothing to be ashamed about."

I can tell he wants me to look at him, but I'm still swallowing the ocean and looking at the pavement.

"Listen," he says. And then he stands up and yells, out toward the street and the building on the other side of it, "I killed two men in the war and every single day I think of their families! One time, I stole food from a grocery store in North Carolina because I was hungry! When my kids were young, I used to spank them even though they were only doing kid stuff! Sometimes I feel like I was a bad husband because I had all this shame!"

By this time, he's standing on the curb and has his arms out.

"Grandad!" I yell. "Stop!"

He turns around and says, "There was one night I left your gram because I thought she deserved better than me. I will never forget the look on her face." He starts to cry. I feel so embarrassed and yet—something else. "She looked disappointed, and I realized I *was* a disappointment. She said, 'Marcus, you have two choices. You can face all this stuff and stay or you can keep running from it and leave.' And let me tell you, Mac, I stayed."

"Wow," I say.

"Are you hearing me?"

"Did you really kill two men?" I ask.

"It was war. It's what war is about."

"Do you really think of their families every day?"

At this, Grandad starts wailing. I mean like a toddler in a grocery store. He's not quiet, he's not curled up in bed. He's on a city street, strangers walking up and down the sidewalks. I stand up and go to him and hug him. We end up back on the bench, straddling it, and he keeps crying.

When he finally gets control of his breath again, he says, "Your turn."

I don't know what to say.

He holds my head so I have to look at him. Tears run down his cheeks, but he's smiling. At me. Nodding a little like he's cheering me on. I think of Dad. I've never seen him cry. And that makes me cry.

"Your turn," he says again.

"I don't like myself," I say. "I think no one else likes me, either. And I think that if someone likes me, they won't like me for long because I'm probably like Dad, even though I don't think I'm like Dad. I don't ever want to get married and I'll probably be a crappy father like he is."

Grandad doesn't move. No hug. No comment. He just waits for more.

"Uh—I am sick of having to fight about dumb stuff like history! Or censored books! I can't stand people who don't want to learn new things! Why do they treat kids like we don't mean anything? I can't even make a difference. Not in my school or the world. I'll never make a difference!"

I look up at Grandad and he's still cheering me on and crying and smiling and it's kinda weird, so I look back down again.

"I like Marci but I don't know what to do about it. She's so cool. I'm not smart enough for her. Denis told Marci about how Dad left and now I don't know what to do. How am I supposed to know what to do? And he's probably mad at me because I got all mad and yelled at him. He didn't even try to fix it. Like I didn't even matter!"

I take a few deep breaths. I realize I'm crying, too, now.

"And I hate my dad!" I say. "He lied to me and to my mom and to everyone he ever knew and I never want to see him again! Nobody likes me or wants me, and if I ran away tomorrow, no one would even care!"

"Whoa, Mac. That's a lot," Grandad says.

"And I think I'll never grow up to be as cool as my grandad because he fought in a war and he has confidence I'll never have! My confidence is fake."

"It is not," he says.

"The only reason I fight against Columbus Day is because it makes me sound smart," I say.

"You are smart."

"I'm smart up here," I say, pointing to my head. "But the rest of me is a mess!"

"We're all a mess," he assures me.

"I don't like being a mess," I answer.

"We're all a mess," he repeats. "The biggest lie ever told to children is that the adults around them aren't a mess."

"All of them?" I ask.

"Most of them, anyway. I don't know anyone who wasn't a mess at some point in their lives. Anyone who says they weren't is lying."

I don't know why this makes me cry harder. I think it's because the truth is beautiful and like rain—it washes everything.

"Let's go get something to eat," Grandad says.

I don't want to get up. I feel like I could do this all day and into the night. "I have more to say!"

"Nothing we can't talk about over a good sandwich," he says. And then he hugs me so tight and I wipe my snot on his shirt and he laughs and wipes his snot on my shirt and then the clouds give way to the sun and the whole scene is over.

I don't know what just happened, but I know everything is different.

BLT

Grandad always orders a BLT. I usually order a grilled cheese, but today I order a BLT, too. I don't even like tomatoes, but the sandwich is the best thing I've ever eaten.

"You can use my phone to call Denis on the ride home," Grandad says.

"Thanks."

"And how about you let me and your mom help you more with this censorship thing? We won't take over—but having us behind you will help. Plus, I know a bunch of guys who fought like I did for your right to read whatever the heck word you want. You need to know when to ask for help."

"I'm sorry you think about those families every day," I say.

He takes a big bite of his BLT. Chews. Nods. The look on his face is something I can't describe. "The best I can do is use my life for something good. Not just for other people. For me, too. Your gram taught me that."

"She was a great lady," I say.

"She was. She made me care about myself."

When I think about it, that's exactly what Grandad just did for me. In public. On a city street. In the rain.

On the way home I call Denis. And I sniffle into the phone like it's no big deal. I tell him how sorry I am for saying the stuff I did. I tell him I don't care that he told Marci.

"Just ask her to the dance," Denis says. "That'll help with some of your stress, right?"

"I don't even know how to do that," I say.

Grandad leans into the phone. "I'll explain it to him, Denis."

I swat him away from the phone. "I've been putting it off the whole week," I say.

"I'll teach him!" Grandad says loudly, tapping his fingertips on his knees.

Denis laughs into the phone. We say goodbye. I say

sorry one more time and he says, "We're best friends, dude. I get it. I'm here for you. Just ask."

I feel like he's giving me a free shot because my dad left.

And then I think he's really cool for giving me the free shot.

I need it.

Grandad teaches me how to ask Marci to the dance. "It's simple. Just ask."

Then he says he's going to dial her number and I ask, "How do you even have her number?"

"We traded at the protest last week."

"So you have my potential girlfriend's number but I don't even have a phone?"

"That's accurate," he says. Then he burps. Then I burp. The BLT was worth it.

When Marci picks up, I say, all in one breath, "Hi, Marci, it's Mac and I want to ask if you'll go to the dance with me on Friday."

She says, "Heck yes!"

And then neither of us knows what to say, so I say that I'm on a bus and it's loud, so I'll talk to her Monday. She says goodbye, and I can hear that she's happy. I'm smiling so big that I know I'm happy.

I guess that's the point.

I look at Grandad and he's smiling, too.

At dinner, things feel different. It's weird to not have seen Dad in two whole weeks. Last time I asked Grandad about his stolen car, he said he was leaving it in the hands of the police. I haven't talked to Mom at all about it. She seems happy, too.

We eat dinner on a Saturday any time we want now.

Waiting . . . and Waiting . . . and Waiting

I
t's the longest week of my life. Denis and I play BOT
DUCK MAN so much, my elbows are sore. But good
things are happening.

On Tuesday after school, Denis and Marci come to
my house and we hang out in the now-empty garage.
Denis tells me I should fix my bike so we can ride the
new bike trails together. Then Marci asks if she can put
music on and she puts on Patti Smith, which is punk
rock. Grandad comes upstairs and pretends to yell at
us for playing the music so loud, but really he came
upstairs to dance with us. We thrash around in the space
left from Dad's spaceship . . . also known as the car
he stole.

As Patti Smith sings "Free Money," Denis tells us he's going to the dance on Friday as friends with Hoa, and Marci and I admit we're relieved because we didn't want to be there without him.

On Tuesday night, the school board announces there's going to be an emergency board meeting next Tuesday. Apparently the local paper isn't the only place people have been arguing about the black rectangles.

At lit circle on Wednesday, Aaron tells us his dad is going to go to the meeting and speak. Then Hoa says *her* parents are coming to the board meeting. I say I'm positive my mom and grandad will come with me, too.

Aaron asks, "What about your dad?" Looks right at me.

I shake my head.

"What?" Aaron says, sensing something off in my response. "Did your dad die or something?"

"Aaron, that's mean," Marci says.

"Sorry," he says. "I'm just curious."

"Well, some people's dads do actually die, so maybe you could be nicer about it," Marci says. "Seriously."

"I don't know where he is," I manage.

"I did not know this." Aaron's face gets stuck in thought.

I try to ignore him and read the book, but I can feel a comment coming any second.

The comment doesn't come until right after recess on Thursday.

We all bring jackets now that it's not so hot, and when we come in from recess and I put mine on my hook in my cubby, Aaron says to the kid he's talking to, "See that kid there? His dad didn't even want him."

I turn around and say, "Shut up, Aaron."

"Well, it's true," he says. "He probably left because you—" This is when Ms. Sett steps in and tugs on Aaron's sweatshirt sleeve. She pulls him out of the classroom and comes back by herself about four minutes later.

The thing is, I want to know what he was going to say next. I want to know the reason he was going to give for my dad doing what he did. Because frankly, I'd really like some ideas.

When lit circle starts, Ms. Sett asks me to come out to the hallway with her.

She says, "I'm sorry for what was said to you today after recess. I've removed Aaron from your group, and you and he will talk during club block later."

"Talk?" I ask.

"Well, he'll apologize," she says.

I nod.

"Are you okay?" she asks.

"Sure," I say.

"Mac. Seriously. You don't stick up for yourself. Why?"

I shrug.

"Has he done it before?" she asks. "Is there anything else I need to know?"

I shake my head. I'm not sure what to do with Ms. Sett being nice. I can't find words.

"You're a smart kid. You have a lot to say. You're doing great. I know home is a bit complicated, but that's no reason to stop believing in yourself," she says. "You're not the same person as you were only a few weeks ago."

"Okay," I manage.

"You're one of our strongest voices. I saw you at that school board meeting. You did so well," she says.

This seems weird because I was speaking against her. I must look confused, because she smiles and laughs a little.

"It's rare to be someone with something to say, Mac. Remember how special you are. Let me know if Aaron bullies you again. And don't forget to have some fun before middle school, okay? If you're serious all the time, that can be hard on your brain."

"Okay," I say. "Thanks."

"I mean it," she says.

"Okay," I say again.

She ruffles my hair on our way into the room.

Thirty minutes later, I'm in Dr. McKenny's office and Aaron James is in front of her desk apologizing to me and I just keep thinking about how Ms. Sett said that I was special and how I had something to say.

"So, I'm sorry. It was rude and I'm sorry about your dad, too," Aaron says.

I let silence gallop by for a moment.

"He's a complicated guy, so it's kinda better this way," I say.

Dr. McKenny does that tilt-nod-impressed-smirk move adults do.

"Yeah, but it's hard to be without a dad," Aaron says.

"It is. I have my grandad, though. He's great."

"That's good."

We both look at Dr. McKenny.

She tells us to go back to Ms. Sett's room, and when we do, we see that Ms. Sett has moved Aaron's desk out of the pod and off on its own, next to our cubbies.

■

By Friday, with the dance ten hours away, it feels like time is standing still. We all just lived the longest week of our lives. The only thing that saves us from going time-crazy is reading the last chapter of *The Devil's Arithmetic*.

But here's what I see: Aaron James, still sitting at a desk of his own over by the coat cubbies, has tears in his eyes. I'm glad Ms. Sett made him think about what he did and apologize, but I also wish he'd been able to do the final day of reading in lit circle with us, not at an isolated desk.

Maybe this makes me too nice. So what? Then I'm too nice. Maybe it makes me a pushover. Whatever. Then I'm a pushover. If I got rid of all my feelings so I could be a mean person, I don't think I could ever forgive myself.

Author Mail

When I check my email during club block, I find a reply from Jane Yolen. This is not what I ever expected.

Dear Mac,

Thank you for contacting me about your experience with censorship of *The Devil's Arithmetic*. Aren't grown-ups strange?

I've written more than four hundred books and I've had some weird things happen. Some people burned a copy of my *Briar Rose* on the steps of the Kansas City Board of Education one time. It was a story of the

Holocaust and included a gay character. So censorship
is not a stranger to me. I am sorry your school is trying
to keep you from perfectly normal words. I am glad you
are working to fix the problem.

I'm also sorry to hear about your dad breaking your mom's
mug. That must be hard. Some people have a lot of anger.
I'm glad you're channeling yours in the right direction.

Remember, Mac, that sometimes we lose the fight.
Don't let it discourage you. There will be other fights
that you will win.

My best,
Jane Yolen

I reply to her right away.

Dear Ms. Yolen,

Thank you for writing back to me!

I'm sorry they burned your book. I don't understand
how people can't see that hating something that much

is bad for them. My grandad says most people are running from shame.

We found out that it was our teacher who censored our books. She didn't think reading the word "breasts" was good for her classroom and said the girls would feel uncomfortable and the boys would laugh. I have a friend named Marci and she says that this is why we need feminism—because small thinking like this limits girls to being embarrassed for normal things like their bodies, and it limits boys from growing up and getting more mature. I think she's right.

We didn't get new reading copies from the school, and the school board is meeting again next Tuesday to decide what to do. In the meantime my grandad bought me a new copy so I could read the book the way you wrote it.

Thanks again for writing back to me. You didn't have to do that, but you did. I really loved the book, by the way. I mean, it was so hard to read about the Holocaust but it's always good to learn the truth of things. That's my mission in life. To teach the truth of things.

I think lies are the same as crossing out words in a book. I mean, isn't it a lie to think you know better than everyone else?

Sincerely,
Mac Delaney

I proofread my reply and hit SEND. I feel bad for not sharing any of this with Marci and Denis but they didn't know about the first letter anyway, and even though they know my dad left town, I still don't want to tell them about the mug.

The Dance

Marci is shy about being in a dress.

"You look great," I say.

"I know," she replies.

"Why do you look so shy?" I ask.

"Some kid already asked me why I'm not wearing a suit," she says.

I look at her like I don't know what she means.

"People think weird stuff about feminists. It's so unnecessary. Like—my dad told me that if I'm a feminist, I won't get any doors opened for me or any flowers from my future husband or whatever. He said that boys won't kiss me because I'm a feminist."

"Feminists want equal rights, fair pay, and stuff like

that," I say. "Right? I mean—what does that have to do with opening doors?"

"Exactly nothing. It makes no sense. People think that because I talk about equal rights, I want to be a man."

"That's a totally different thing," I say. "Like—a totally different thing!"

"I know. But it's what people think."

We stand outside the gym doors, and other kids walk by us to get in and start dancing or whatever people do at a dance.

I want to ask Marci if she'll hold my hand but my hands are so sweaty, I can't. Instead, I open my mouth and weird words come out.

"You know, I think you're pretty. And really smart," I say.

"I think you're the smartest and coolest person I know. And you're really cute," she responds, smiling.

I'm grinning so hard I can't keep my teeth in.

Denis shows up wearing a pair of suit pants made into shorts. Marci and I look at the shorts and smile.

"Punk rock," he says. "Have you seen Hoa?"

We both shake our heads.

"Go inside," he tells us. "We'll be in when she gets here."

Marci and I go in and get back to smiling at each other.

She says, "I really want to have fun tonight. Like—real fun." And right when she says that, Aaron James shows up and puts his arms around both of us. He smells like salami and lime deodorant.

"I made a bunch of requests for slow songs so you love-birds can kiss and stuff," he says. Then he laughs and walks over to a crowd of boys who have no dates.

"I still can't tell if he really thinks the Earth is flat or not," Marci says. "But I don't really care, either."

"Yeah," I say. "Wanna dance?"

We go to the gym floor, which isn't as full as I'd like it to be.

Marci says, "I wish they played punk rock."

"Me too!" I say, and start dancing as if the pop song they're playing is actually punk rock.

She starts, too. And soon we're just bouncing around to songs we both don't know the words to. It's fun. I'm sweating and I don't even care. After a while, I notice Marci is sweating and she doesn't care, either.

The kids-with-no-dates are all out on the dance floor, doing some kind of boys-in-a-circle dance, and then "Rock Lobster" comes on and only a few people know to drop to the floor and do the whole lobster thing, and Marci and I are doing it and then the kids-with-no-dates do it, too, and it's not like everything is perfect now, but it's better.

Everything is better now.

Until I remember Denis.

When "Rock Lobster" is over, I look around for Hoa and she's not here, either. I tell Marci. She looks around, too, and then says, "Let's go find them." She takes my hand and we walk out of the gym.

Denis and Hoa are definitely not in the school building. We look everywhere twice. Mr. Singer is on door duty and he says, "Are your parents here to pick you up?"

"No," I say. "We just need to go out to find a friend."

"Once you go out, you can't come back in," he says.

Marci says, "That's a weird rule. We're hot. I'm sweating. I just want to get some air."

"Yeah," I say.

He makes a gesture like he doesn't want to get caught. "Okay—but stay where I can see you."

We go out. Marci says, "I'll stay here and cool off. You go find them."

I run all the way around the school building. I do my secret call for Denis—like a red-tailed hawk—and there's no answer. I don't have a phone, so I can't call him. But I'm worried. He was all dressed and ready and seemed excited to come in.

When I get back to Marci, I say, "I couldn't find either Denis or Hoa."

"We should go to Denis's house," she says. "But I have to go home and change out of this dress first."

She opens the school door and tells Mr. Singer we're walking home. He seems surprised but distracted and waves us off.

Popcorn

By the time Marci and I get to her house so she can put jeans on, and then back to Denis's house, it's eight forty-five. We ring the doorbell, and at first we think no one is home, but then I see Denis peeking through the living room window.

"Hi!" I say.

He comes to the door.

"What are you guys doing here?" he asks.

"You weren't at the dance. We were worried," Marci says.

I can tell from his expression that he's sad.

"What happened, dude?"

"I don't want to talk about it."

Marci says, "Can we come in? We can eat popcorn or

something. That always helps." Denis lets us come in and we stand in the living room.

"Did Hoa show up?" I ask.

After a few more attempts to get an answer, Denis flops down on the couch and says, "She showed up. We were going to go in. But then—"

Denis looks like he's going to cry. Marci and I sit on the couch next to him and tell him it's going to be okay. Finally, he says, "She likes me. Like—she *likes* me likes me."

"Oh," Marci says.

"It's okay. Hoa is really nice," I say.

"That's the problem!" Denis says. "She's so nice and I had to make her feel bad."

"You probably didn't make her feel that bad. We're in sixth grade. It's not like you left her standing at the altar on your wedding day or anything," Marci says.

"Not helping!" Denis groans.

"You told her you were going to the dance as friends," I say. "You can't do more than that. Hoa will be fine. She's so cool. Come on. Stop feeling bad."

We make popcorn and sit around the kitchen table.

"I feel like a weirdo," Denis says.

"Because you don't get crushes?" Marci asks. "A lot of people are aro, ace, or aroace. You're not alone."

Aroace means: a person who doesn't experience romantic or sexual attraction.

"True," Denis answers.

I ask, "So where did Hoa go? Why didn't you just come dance with us?"

He shakes his head. "She said she didn't want to go in. She's shy, you know? I said I'm shy, too, so we decided to just walk around town a little. We got ice cream and then I walked her home and came here."

"We've all had crushes that don't crush back," Marci says. "Hoa will get over it."

"I guess I wish she didn't have to," Denis says.

"Dude, you can't live like that," I say. "You're a great person and there's nothing wrong with you not crushing on people. We're twelve. Come on. This stuff is for later. Or maybe never. You be you—whatever the case, Marci's right: You're not alone."

"Hold on—where are your parents?" Marci asks.

"On a dinner date. Should be home soon," he says.

"Why don't we take a night walk?" I suggest.

Marci and I call home to explain where we are so they won't head to the school to pick us up from the dance. Then the three of us head out, taking the popcorn bowl with us. Marci stuffs a napkin into her back pocket. We walk from Denis's house to Main Street, and then when we cross Main to head to the railroad tracks, there's a weird noise behind us. *Bwip-Bwip.*

It's a police car.

With its lights on.

Denis stops and looks at the sidewalk. Inside, he is freaking out and I know it. I stand in front of him and cross my arms. Marci keeps eating popcorn. The police officer smiles at us.

"You're Marcus's grandkid!" the guy says. "The protester."

I nod.

"It's past curfew," he says. "You shouldn't be walking around."

Marci points to a group of people leaving the restaurant half a block down, and to three women walking on the other side of the street. "But—"

"Just get yourselves home," he says.

"We were taking a night walk," I say. "We only just got started."

"Sorry to cut it short, but you have to get home," the officer says. "Unless you want me to drive you."

Denis sighs. I roll my eyes. Marci keeps eating popcorn.

We walk Denis home first and Marci washes the

popcorn bowl and hugs Denis goodbye. Then I walk Marci home. When we get close to her house, we stop holding hands. She pauses on the sidewalk and looks at me.

"I don't think I want to kiss anybody until I'm older."

"Me neither," I say.

She blows a relieved breath out of her mouth and puffs out her cheeks. "Oh good."

I walk her to her front door. She thanks me for the nice night, and I turn around and head home. Grandad is waiting for me, and I tell him about the dance and the interrupted stroll.

That night, I sleep so well, Grandad has to wake me up to go protest.

He has a new sign.

LET PEOPLE WALK AROUND, OKAY?

Trick or Treat

I want us to rethink the rules around Halloween and an official trick-or-treat night. I don't understand why the borough board had to be so rash in their decision when they canceled it, but I wish they would have asked parents in town. Or kids. Because no kid wants to cancel Halloween.

—Edith Jackson, Cherry Lane

Re: Trick or Treat

There are worse things than not being able to ring strangers' doorbells in the dark and collect free junk food. While I remember the joys of trick-or-treating myself, I don't think it's worth putting children at risk for a little candy.

—Laura Samuel Sett

Columbus Boy

There's poster paper and markers on the kitchen table when I come downstairs in the morning, so I decide to make a new sign, too. Then I make another one. And another. I have so many things to say.

Grandad grabs the folding chairs from the garage where his car is still missing, and I put on my sneakers.

Mom arrives in a T-shirt I've never seen before. It says, *Don't be scared. I'm just a feminist.* She says, "Are we eating first? Or do you want to get something while we're out? That new place on Main has great breakfast sandwiches."

I don't know why I'm so shocked that Mom is here.

"What's wrong?" she asks.

"Nothing," I say.

"I don't have to come with you if you don't want. I get that this is your thing with your grandfather."

"No!" I say. "I want you to come. I'm just not used to—uh."

"You're used to her being here on Saturday, cooped up all day and making dinner for spaceman Mike," Grandad says.

Mom scolds him for being sarcastic.

"Sorry, but the man stole my car," he says.

She doesn't say anything else. She doesn't have to. I can see it in her face.

"You didn't do anything wrong," I tell her. "You tried. You even still let him come over and made him dinner!"

"I just wish it would have worked out," she says.

"He smashed your blue mug," I say. "Nothing you could have done."

"Hear, hear," Grandad adds.

"It's been a long time since I've been to a protest," Mom says.

"I brought licorice shoestrings." Grandad holds up his candy bag.

Mom smiles and looks like she's going to cry. Those are her favorite.

We walk until we get to the space in front of Tad's where we sit every Saturday. It's finally feeling like autumn, and I'm not sweating for once. Grandad and I set out the chairs and Mom goes to buy us breakfast sandwiches.

"Nice sign," Grandad says.

I smile and balance it on my knees. It's my favorite.

CENSORSHIP: WHEN GROWN-UPS ACT LIKE CHILDREN!

"Is that Marci?" Mom asks as she carries two cups of coffee in a cup carrier and a brown paper bag in her other hand. She's looking behind me, so I turn around.

"Hi!" Marci says.

"Hey," I answer. I get up and set her chair out next to mine.

"What do you think?" she asks, showing me a colorful sign that says STOP BEING AFRAID OF WORDS with a stop sign as the O in STOP.

"Love it," I say. I turn my sign around to show her the other side.

She smiles. "Always one step ahead, Mac."

STEALING HALLOWEEN FROM CHILDREN? SOUNDS LIKE A TRICK TO ME.

"That's my boy," Mom says.

I offer Marci half my breakfast sandwich and we sit down and eat. Grandad's friends always stop and say hello. They keep laughing at my sign, saying when they were kids, things were a lot more "loose" around town.

"We could walk around and do whatever we wanted," one says.

Marci has small leaflets that she's handing out. On the front, it's an overview of what happened with our copies of *The Devil's Arithmetic* with a picture of the blacked-out part. On the back is the proposed school board policy.

A woman who passed by and took a leaflet a half hour before comes to us and says, "It's sad that this is happening. I'd love to help."

Marci says, "The best way to help is to come to the emergency board meeting on Tuesday night. You can sign up to speak or just bring a sign!"

The woman says, "Sounds good. I'll be there."

Only after she's long gone, Grandad says, "She's Tony Farisi's daughter."

"Isn't that the guy who started the bookstore?"

"Sanctimonious turd," he says.

"Yeah, him," I answer.

"She turned out a lot nicer than her old man. And a lot

smarter about the world. I hear she's running for school board," Grandad says.

"I bet she really meant it, then," Marci comments.

More people than usual stop to talk to us. All of them support our cause. It makes me feel nervous. I know there are people who don't agree. I guess they're keeping to themselves. We've been here three hours already and we decide to stay longer. The place is packed because it's a beautiful day.

"Columbus boy!" someone says. I know the voice. It's Aaron James.

He's with a man who I assume is his dad. The man says, "Nice sign!" I'm a bit surprised Aaron's dad likes my sign, but he's only seen the Halloween side, so who can't get behind that?

Aaron and his dad talk for a while with Marci, who gives them leaflets, and I talk to a woman who stops to say she's behind us all the way. Grandad tells her about the meeting, but she says she can't make it. "Write a letter to the board," he says. "And to the paper!"

"That, I can do!" she answers. "Good luck!"

Aaron and Aaron's dad go to the bookstore, and Aaron comes out with a copy of *The Devil's Arithmetic*. He shows it to me, smiling.

"But we already finished reading it," I say.

His dad says, "Don't worry. I'm billing the school district for it!"

Grandad laughs. I don't see why that's funny. When Aaron and his dad leave, Grandad explains. "Some people go about protesting in different ways. I'm pretty sure that guy and I don't vote for the same people, but we think the same about our kids. And grandkids. You get my drift."

"I'll take whatever support I can get," Marci says.

I nod.

By the time three o'clock rolls around, we're all hungry and Mom suggests we drop the chairs back home and go to the sandwich shop. I ask if Marci can come with us.

"Can I call my mom and see if that's okay?" Marci asks. She borrows Grandad's phone and comes with us.

My hands aren't sweaty around her anymore. She's just my friend, only a bit more. I've known her forever. She knows how to dance to "Rock Lobster." We are fighting a town together.

When we get to the sandwich shop, I order a grilled cheese kid's meal and so does Marci. When the food comes and we start eating, she says, "I don't know how you eat French fries without ketchup."

I say, "And I don't know how you eat French fries *with* ketchup."

Suddenly, Grandad jumps out of the booth we're sitting in and runs toward the window.

"That's my car!" he yells.

And then he runs out the door and down Main Street.

Karmann Ghia Convertible

Grandad is a fast runner for a man his age. Plus, tourists don't tend to use the dedicated crosswalks in town on Saturdays, so traffic can be slow. By the time Marci, Mom, and I get outside, Grandad has already caught up with the car and is yelling something at my dad, who is in the driver's seat.

From what it looks like, Dad is ignoring Grandad and pretending it's his car. That's an educated guess on my part—I'm too far away to see or hear what's really going on.

"I'm calling about a physical altercation on Main Street," Mom says into her phone. "If they just walk out of the office, they'll hear it."

It's true. If the police step out their door, they'll have front-row seats to whatever is about to happen.

As I get closer, I can hear what Grandad is saying. "Block the car!" he's saying to anyone who'll listen. "This is my car!"

Two older guys step in front of the car so Dad can't drive forward. Grandad stands with his arms crossed and says something quietly to Dad. Dad keeps looking forward as if Grandad isn't standing there.

"You okay?" Marci asks.

I nod. "My dad is in the long grass," I tell her. I don't even care if she understands. I know what I'm talking about.

"But you're okay?" she asks.

"I'm embarrassed," I say.

We start to walk toward the car. The police arrive at the same time and ask my dad to pull the car into the nearby bank's drive-through lane. Mom is now standing next to Grandad.

Dad gets out of the car and says something I can't hear. Then he . . . walks away. The police go to stop him but Grandad puts his hand out and says something while he shakes his head. Dad takes off running up Broad Street. Running.

I walk over to Mom. She ruffles my hair. I say, "I worry about him."

She says, "Me too. But he's his own man and he can't

seem to see what he's doing to us or himself. And it's not our problem to solve."

I look into the car. On the floor of the back seat is my old baseball glove.

The police go back to what they were doing and the four of us pile into the car and drive the four blocks home. Grandad leaves the Karmann Ghia in the driveway so he can wash it. He opens the trunk, which is in front, where the engine usually is, and finds a bunch of our stuff. My baseball bag is there, and he tosses it to me. I find my lucky rock and put it in my pocket.

I walk Marci home.

"That was . . . confusing," she says.

"Yeah. My dad is confusing."

A lot of silence goes by. Too much.

"Let's focus on the board meeting," she says. She holds my hand and squeezes it. "It's better to think about things you can control instead of things you can't control. And all that adult stuff is up to the adults."

"I'm not looking forward to the board meeting," I say. "I have a bad feeling that they aren't going to do the right thing."

"All we can do is give them a good fight."

"That's what Jane Yolen said when she wrote back to

me," I say. But then I remember. "Oh shoot. I never told you that story."

"Wrote back? Does this mean you wrote to her?"

So I tell Marci that I sent a letter and that, yes, Jane Yolen wrote back. "I'll show it to you," I say. Then I realize I have to tell Marci the mug story. And when I tell her, she looks sad. "Anyway," I conclude, "even if we lose this fight, we just keep fighting."

The way Marci talks for the rest of the walk is all grace. She's not mad at me for not sharing my letter with her and Denis, and when we arrive at her house, she gives me a hug that has all kinds of grace in it. She says, "Don't worry. Your dad will figure himself out one day. And if he doesn't, he's missing out on the coolest kid I ever met."

Lighter / Heavier / Lighter

I walk home from Marci's and think of all the ridiculous rules in town and try to number them in order of priority. For me, censorship, dress codes, and curfew are of the highest importance. Then junk food. Then Halloween.

Grandad and Mom are on the front porch when I get home, and I ask them, "Are we still going to get my bike ready?" Grandad nods and smiles. So I go to the garage.

I get my bike and turn it upside down, balancing it on its handlebars and seat. I spin the wheels. I have no idea how to fix a bike outside of pumping up the tires, but I know Grandad does and I know it's not really broken, just a little run-down.

When I walk over to the bench to get the tire pump,

that's when I see Dad, sitting on an upturned five-gallon bucket—the same one I'd sit on when I helped him work on his "spacecraft." He waves. As if that's a normal thing to do.

I feel a sort of panic rise in me and then I remember what Marci just said about how I'm the coolest kid she knows. I take a deep breath like Grandad would.

"Hi, Dad," I say.

"I had to stick up for myself, kid."

I don't even know what to say, so I keep breathing deep and I start to connect the pump to my bike tire.

"What?" he says. "What aren't you saying?"

I let seconds run by. Then I say, "You had to stick up for yourself to who? Mom? All she ever did was go to work, help people, make us food to eat, clean up after us, and love us."

"I had to stick up for—I had to make my voice heard," he says.

"We all heard you just fine."

"You're listening to your grandfather now."

"He has a lot of good stuff to say." I start to pump the tire up. "And he doesn't change stories around so he's the hero. Or the victim. Not even the war stories. He's honest. Even if it makes him look bad. I'm a lot like him."

"I guess you are." Dad says this like it's not a good thing.

More seconds run by.

"Can I ask you a question?" I venture.

"Sure," he says.

"What are you so ashamed of?"

"What?!"

"I said, what are you so ashamed of?"

"I'm not ashamed of anything!" he shouts.

I look at him. He looks at me.

"Listen," I say. "I don't think anyone likes me and I'm not smart enough to be Marci's boyfriend or I didn't think I was, and now I don't know what I think. I sometimes think I'll never be able to be happy with a girlfriend anyway. I'm scared of relationships and—"

"Stop, Mac," Dad says.

"And I don't know why you smashed Mom's mug and I'm embarrassed that you did and that you took our stuff and left, and I'm tired of adults lying to kids and—"

"No!" Dad interrupts. Then he stands up, looks at me without understanding me at all, and says, "You gotta stop living in the past."

I don't let this stop me. "Also, I feel really bad about the way I treated Denis last weekend and I think it will take him a while to trust me again. I don't blame him. I was a jerk to him."

"What are you trying to prove?" Dad asks.

I don't have an answer. I notice I'm shaking. I can't tell if I'm scared or angry or cold but I think it might be all three. Dad doesn't move. He looks past me to the garage door switch, then back at me. He's trapped. I can't move, so I'm trapped, too.

Grandad solves the problem by opening the garage door from the outside and then saying, "Mike. Fancy seeing you in my garage."

"I was just leaving," Dad says. "Wanted to stop by and see Mac." He turns back to me. "Okay, bud. So I'll be in touch about the camping trip and stuff."

I have never been camping with my father. I'm not sure he's ever been camping himself. And now he's more like an alien than he ever was except, actually, he's always been like this. Always acts half-caught, like what he's doing is wrong. Always throws out weird lies like *I'll be in touch about camping!* that make me feel like a disposable accomplice.

I'm glad Marci said those nice things about me earlier because those things are what's holding me together right now. Between that and Grandad's deep breaths, I feel like I'm pretty okay.

By the time I look up from my bike, still spinning the pedal so I can feel the tire running across my fingers, Dad is gone and Grandad stands, smiling at me. Or maybe it's more of a grimace.

"I don't even know what to say to you, Mac," he says.

I nod and keep spinning the pedal.

"I'm going to keep trying to help him figure out—" He stops talking when I put my hand up.

I say, "Some battles we lose. Some battles we win. But some battles aren't ours to fight."

Grandad moves over to the bench and gets the oilcan. We grease the bike's gears and chain, we check the tires again, we wipe it down and clean it until our hands are black.

Letters to the Editor—Snippets

Re: Junk Food—You may buy all the junk food you like and eat it whenever you like. If you don't like living here anymore, move somewhere else!

I started thinking about how the person who censored these books is the same person who helped push the ordinance against pizza delivery. I would like to get pizza delivered sometimes and I don't think there's anything wrong with that.

Last Saturday, I talked to the kids who complained about the book that was censored. They were kind, intelligent, well-spoken, and determined. I think without knowing it, our school system just created a bunch of kids who will care more about the real world than my generation ever did. Go, kids! We stand with you!

If they're censoring fiction books in this district, how do we know if they're censoring history books? Science? How do we know what's really being taught?

I know it's not holiday time yet, but I'd like to remind people in the district that it's not right or legal for our school to put on a holiday show with religious music. If we're so strict as to not allow junk food or certain words in books, then why are we allowing this religious show and forcing children who do not believe in this religion to sing about it?

Halloween

Three years ago, some guy walked around on trick-or-treat night wearing a scary mask and holding a rubber knife. He was older—maybe a college kid or even someone my dad's age. Probably just trying to get in the spirit. But he scared a bunch of little kids and parents, too, so they decided that if we stopped having Halloween, that would solve the problem.

All it did was make kids sad not to be able to trick-or-treat and eat free candy.

Turns out, censorship is never the right decision.

The last thing on our mind Monday is trick-or-treating, though. Marci has printed agendas for the five minutes we've been given to speak at the emergency board meeting tomorrow. She hands a copy to me and Aaron and sticks the rest of them in her back pocket.

"My dad is going first," she says. "Then Aaron's dad."

Hoa says, "My parents can't make it, but they wrote them a letter."

"My mom wants to say a few things," I say.

"Yep," Marci says. "I talked to her last night. She goes last."

We sit in our desk pod with our censored books in front of us. I had to bring mine back in to return it, but I want to save the censored one as a memento, so I plan on giving Ms. Sett my uncensored one.

Aaron has been allowed back into the pod. Ms. Sett starts going from pod to pod, asking groups what they thought of their books. Until it's our turn, we talk about random stuff.

"You guys were right. I liked the book," Aaron says. This makes Hoa smile.

I say, "If you liked this one, I have two that you might really love at home. Part time travel, part mystery. I have a bunch of manga, too."

Aaron nods.

"You can walk home with me if you want and borrow them," I offer.

"Sounds good. Can't do it tonight, though. Going to the haunted house," he says.

"What haunted house?" Marci asks.

"It's secret. My friends would kill me if I told you."

"We *are* your friends," Hoa says.

After a minute, Aaron tells us where the haunted house is. It's only a few blocks from Denis's house.

"That place?" Denis says. "It's not haunted. It's infested with squirrels."

"Ghost squirrels," Aaron says.

When she gets to group four, Ms. Sett surprises us all with the offer of Halloween treats. "Hoa, can you go to the closet and get the big grocery bag I put in there?"

Hoa goes to the closet and Aaron keeps talking about the haunted house. "They hire real prisoners to scare you—like murderers and stuff!" I watch Ms. Sett talk to group four about their book and she seems so good at her job. And yet here I am, holding a censored book.

"Mac!" Hoa whispers.

I look over and she gives me the signal to come to the closet.

Aaron and Denis are now debating whether real prisoners could be actors in a haunted house. Marci is reading over her list of things to do before tomorrow's meeting.

Ms. Sett is engaged in whatever conversation is happening in group four.

I slide out of my chair and slowly walk over. Hoa hands me the big bag of Halloween snacks—sugar-free fruit snacks, of course—and says, "Look."

She holds a book open to a page with another black rectangle. It's not *The Devil's Arithmetic*. It's a different book.

"All of these have them," she says, pointing to a box.

I pull one out and zip through the pages quickly, stopping at a place where so much of the page is black rectangles, Ms. Sett should have just ripped out the page.

Hoa says, "I love that book!"

"It won a gold medal," I say.

Hoa takes the book out of my hand and reaches down for two different books, then hands all three of them to me and motions for me to hide them. So I hand her the bag of fruit snacks and hide the books in the waistband of my jeans under my shirt.

When she gets back to group six from delivering the Halloween treats to Ms. Sett—now at group five—I hand her the books and she shoves them into her desk. Denis looks from me to Hoa and back at me. Marci is still reading her agenda for the meeting tomorrow night. Aaron is muttering to himself like he's trying to memorize something.

Then Ms. Sett sits at our desk pod and says, "Well, group six. Tell me what you thought of the book!"

We talk for a minute about the things we read and the things we learned from *The Devil's Arithmetic*. I space out and stare out the window as Denis talks. And then, suddenly, Aaron says, "I think it was a really great detail she wrote in there about the girls covering their breasts because anyone would in that situation, you know?"

Before any of us can say anything, Aaron is in the hallway with Ms. Sett. Then she comes back in and he doesn't. Ms. Sett sits at our table again. She expects us to talk, but we won't.

"What's gotten into you guys?" she asks.

None of us says a word.

She looks sternly at me. I know she stood up for me last week when Aaron was mean to me. I know she was kind. But it still doesn't mean I won't stick up for Aaron. We may be a mismatched team, but we're here for each other.

"Mac, come with me," she says, and heads out to the hallway.

I'm frozen. Not sure what to do. Marci gets up and

goes out instead. Then Denis follows. Then Hoa. So I have no choice but to go, too.

"Start talking," Ms. Sett says.

None of us says anything.

"Fine, go to the office," she says. She walks into the classroom and expects us to do what she says. We don't. Marci has the extra agendas her dad printed in her pocket and a Sharpie marker.

We pass the marker around. Make four signs.

YOU CAN'T CENSOR PEOPLE.

~~BREAST~~ IS JUST A WORD.

SILENT PROTEST IN PROGRESS.

FREE AARON JAMES!

We decide with our eyes to skip club block. Marci can miss a day of chorus. Denis can play chess any time he wants. We sit outside Ms. Sett's room silently holding our signs.

The assistant principal approaches us as the end of the day gets nearer. He tells us to follow him. We don't. He asks us to tell him why we're doing this. We don't. He goes into the room to talk to Ms. Sett and the intercom rings out with the usual bus calls. Suddenly, hallways are filled with kids and a lot of them notice us but don't say anything. Some people stand for a while and read our signs. A little kid smiles and sits down with us.

The assistant principal comes back out of the room along with Ms. Sett.

"You guys have to get up right now and get your things and walk home," he says.

I want to tell him that we're not trying to disrespect him, but I stay quiet. He and Ms. Sett and Mr. Black, the science teacher, and the substitute music teacher who's really cool all stand there looking at us. The walkers are called to leave. Then the last bus. We stay seated and quiet. More kids join us, so there are about ten of us now. I don't even know the other kids here. They just sat down and clammed up.

This is what happens when you take candy from children on Halloween.

When I get home, Grandad is waiting for me on the front porch.

"Did they call Mom?" I ask.

"Sounds like you had a great day!" he answers. "And yeah. They called her. She called me."

"I might be suspended," I say.

"You won't be."

"It feels like a hundred years until tomorrow night and the meeting," I say. "How do you stay calm?"

He pulls two strings of beads from his jacket pocket. His, and . . . mine.

"These are for you," he says. "I've been making this string for the last month. I made sure to get crystals that most matched your personality and your needs. Had to special order that Botswana agate."

"You're a real hippie," I say, taking the beads. I feel bad because I have no intention of meditating.

"My friend Laurie taught me about these. They're really effective. You look pretty worked up right now, so just sit down and let me show you."

I put my backpack on the porch floor next to the other rocking chair and I sit down. I look at the meditation beads he just gave to me. On one end of the string, there's a big clear quartz crystal. On the other end, there's a little charm of a tree. Grandad explains everything. How to use each bead for a breath or a task. When we get to the one where I think of all I'm grateful for, I sit with my eyes closed and get lost in a river of gratitude.

It's funny. When I think of Dad, I'm grateful that he taught me what not to be and what not to do, and I'm grateful that I told him what I really thought of him on Saturday. When I think those things, I feel less like his personal garbage and more like a 100 percent human kid who got unlucky when it comes to my father. That's all.

By the time I work my way up the different crystal beads, I feel so much calmer than I ever thought I would from doing something so easy. All I'm doing is breathing and directing my thoughts.

"I didn't know meditation had anything to do with thinking," I say.

"It does and it doesn't. It really all depends on the day."

"I'm grateful," I say. "Thank you for the beads."

"Take them with you tomorrow night to the meeting. They'll give you confidence and strength. I made sure of it when I made them," he says.

When Mom comes home, we all go inside and talk about what happened at school today. Grandad makes dinner while she sits with her feet up on the couch. She looks so comfortable, I lie the same way on the other couch.

When I wake up, there's a blanket on me. The whole room is dark except for the stove light. Mom's still asleep on her couch and she has a blanket on her, too. There's a note by the stove from Grandad. *When you wake up, if you're hungry, there's food in the fridge. Microwave for a minute on high. Love you.*

When I finally settle onto my bed to sleep again, I bring my new string of beads with me. I stop at the gratitude bead and I fall asleep to memories of me and Grandad over the years. I know my dad is my dad, but Grandad is my father. It's possible to choose. No one can change my mind about that.

Surprise!

School happens. None of us gets suspended. That's all that matters. Nine thousand years pass between school and seven p.m., when the emergency school board meeting starts. I think I might even have a few gray hairs now.

We get to the meeting early and it's already packed with people. Marci, Denis, and I have to squeeze through to the front, and with no chairs left, we opt to sit cross-legged on the floor. I can feel people glaring at us. I'm not sure if it's because they know we're the kids who started this thing or if it's just that we're kids and sitting on the floor. Soon, Grandad appears at the edge of the tightly packed mass of people; he sidles over and sits cross-legged next to us. He has his beads in his hand. I swear he's not ever ashamed of who he is. It makes me sit up taller.

Even Denis stops slouching.

Right when the board is about to call the meeting to order, Hoa pops out of the crowd and smiles at the three of us. Aaron pops out after her. They sit down next to us on the floor. Hoa has the three books from Ms. Sett's closet under her arm. Aaron has the same look as yesterday before the silent protest.

The board knows we're all here about the censored book. They make us wait anyway while they take care of two other "emergency" things relating to parent volunteers and something else I don't hear. I pull out my beads and find the gratitude bead and roll it between my finger and thumb. Marci smiles at me. I smile back. I'm grateful for Marci. She's still the smartest person I know and I like everything about her.

Our time finally comes and Marci's dad starts with a perfectly timed two-minute spiel about policy and intellectual freedom and how organizations like the American Civil Liberties Union (ACLU) and the American Library Association (ALA) have many resources for library and school boards. He also says they have lawyers who work in this field and the board wouldn't want to come up against them.

He's a firecracker, Grandad would say. Marci is beaming.

Aaron's dad is not as well-spoken but he sure is emotional.

"Who does this teacher think she is, choosing what words my son can't read?" he says. "And how come you don't have more control over your own teachers when they get to censoring perfectly good books like these?"

He ends with a statement about freedom and the first amendment and how people died to give us our rights, that the board has no respect for those people who died if they take those rights away. It's very moving. He's good.

Mom makes her way through the crowd. She simply says, "I work with dying people. It's what I do. I help people die. I've talked to some of the people I work with about what happened here and I want to share with you what Lester, who's ninety-five years old, said. Lester told me, 'When you get to death's door, you regret all the things you could have learned but didn't.' I think this board and this town and this teacher have a lot to learn." She smiles. "Thank you."

The board president starts to speak but the crowd is

jostling and people have their hands up and want to talk. Then a small older woman emerges in front. She walks to where the microphone is, but doesn't use it.

"Ladies and gentlemen," she starts.

The board president cuts her off. "I'm sorry, but we don't have any more time for comments."

The woman acts as if the board president hasn't spoken.

"My name is Jane Yolen. I was passing through town and I heard there was a meeting about some of my words tonight. So I decided to stop by."

Most of the people in the room haven't realized that this is the author of the book. They're still raising hands and trying to say things. The board president looks mad. I'm frozen in place.

"When I was a child, and I learned about the Holocaust and what happened to my people, the Jewish people, during the Second World War, I was horrified, like anyone is. But I was also relieved. I was relieved because I was seven years old and the adults around me weren't keeping it a secret. I knew, at that young age, that I could trust them to tell me the truth."

I swear my mouth is hanging open.

Jane Yolen.

Passing through town.

Came to this meeting.

She goes on to say that she wrote the book to give to readers what was given to her: the truth of a terrible, impossible thing. "Six million of my people were murdered. Six million women, men, and children. And this district is crossing out words for body parts? I'm not shocked. But it's funny, don't you think? That you're concerned with a word when six million people died?"

I stand up. I don't know why.

"I've had my books burned and shredded and pulled out of kids' hands. Nothing shocks me anymore. But I'm here to say that children need to learn the truth. The whole picture of it, and not just the parts adults think they're capable of understanding. Our job is to help them understand, not black out the topic."

The room has realized who this is and hands go down. Adults are staring at her or trying to get a look.

"Thanks for giving me some extra time," she says. "Would have been a shame to come all this way and not get to speak up for the capable, intelligent children you are educating. You taught them a lot with this experiment. I believe it's now your turn to learn."

Then she spins around and starts to walk out.

That's when Hoa stands up in front of the nine board

members and says, "Hold on!" She opens a book and reads aloud into the microphone. "'If the peach is leaking then we shall surely sink! Don't be an'—"

Aaron screams, "BLACK RECTANGLE!"

Hoa finishes the sentence. "—'the Centipede told him.' That's *James and the Giant Peach* by Roald Dahl, page one hundred six." She shows the black rectangle to the crowd and hands the book to the board president, who is still holding a gavel in her right hand.

Jane Yolen stands, watching.

Hoa opens another book. "This is page thirteen of Newbery-winning *The Higher Power of Lucky*," she says.

"BLACK RECTANGLE!" Aaron yells.

Hoa jumps right in. "—'sounded to Lucky like something green that comes up when you have the flu and cough too much . . . Deep inside she thought she *would* be interested in *seeing* an actual'—"

"BLACK RECTANGLE!" Aaron yells.

"'But at the same time—and this is where Lucky's brain was very complicated—she definitely did *not* want to see'—"

Aaron yells and Denis joins him. "BLACK RECTANGLE!"

Hoa shows the crowd three pages of black rectangles in the book and hands it to the board president, who is being screeched at by a woman also on the board who thinks the president should stop Hoa from talking. Everyone hears the president when she says, "These are the students you care *so much about*, Emma. I think they should be heard."

Hoa speaks over the exchange. "This is Judy Blume's *Are You There God? It's Me, Margaret*, which has many pages that look like this one." She shows the crowd a page with a few black rectangles on it. "This is from page thirty-five. '"And," Janie added, "she's been"'—"

Aaron and Denis and I yell, "BLACK RECTANGLE!"

Hoa continues, "—'"since fourth grade"'—"

"BLACK RECTANGLE!"

Hoa reads, ""Did you get it yet, Margaret?" Nancy asked. "Get what?"'—"

"BLACK RECTANGLE!" Aaron yells, with help from the crowd. I can hear Grandad in there somewhere. And Mom. And Aaron's dad, who looks so proud. He's recording the whole thing on his phone.

Hoa says, ""Oh—no, not yet. Did you?" Nancy swallowed some'—"

"BLACK RECTANGLE!" the crowd yells.

Hoa goes on, "—'and shook her head. "None of us has yet."'" She takes a deep breath. "These are just a few examples. How many more books will it take? When will it stop if *you* don't stop it?" She takes a small bow in the board's direction, says, "Thank you for your time," and then puts the microphone down.

Jane Yolen smiles at Hoa, turns back toward the door, and walks out.

I follow her.

"Wow!" she says. "You guys know how to throw a meeting!"

I introduce myself and then say, "I didn't even know Hoa was going to do that. Or Aaron."

"It was effective, don't you think?"

"I think so," I say.

We walk to her car and don't say much. I thank her for coming. She tells me that I shouldn't think too much about why my dad does bad things and instead try to find one thing I like about him. I tell her that's a hard one, but I'll try.

"I think you're brave," I say to her.

"I think you're fearless," she says.

Marci and Denis come out of the building and start walking toward us, followed by Hoa and Aaron. Jane Yolen gets in the car and rolls down her window. She introduces me to her friend, who's in the driver's seat.

"Ms. Yolen!" Marci says. "Can I shake your hand?"

Jane smiles all goofy and shakes Marci's hand.

"I loved your book," Marci says. "Uh. Thanks for writing it."

"Me too," Denis says.

"Us too!" Hoa says. Aaron is waving his hand like he's seeing a rock star.

"I'm grateful for you," I say to her.

"Keep in touch," she says. "Keep being yourself." She smiles and the car backs out of the parking space and drives down the road.

"Wow," Marci says.

"Yeah," I say.

"That was so cool," Denis says.

"Yeah," Hoa answers.

We turn and walk back to the entrance. "I wonder if she listens to punk rock," Marci says.

"She seems too old," Denis says.

"A lot of those singers are in their eighties now. You never know," Marci says.

I listen to them talk and know that no matter what happens with the school board or the book or the policy, everything is going to be fine. Middle school will be fine. High school will be fine.

I just need to keep being myself.

What Happens Next

B ecause the paper was getting so many letters, the governing bodies in town, the borough council and the town board, announced two extra meetings for the months of November and December. They would be held in the back room of the Main Street Hotel because the last meeting was so big, it didn't fit in the tiny room in the town hall anymore. People wanted rules changed. Pizza delivery. Blue houses. Halloween. People wanted to live again the way other towns lived. Many adults around here finally realized, maybe, that they have a say in what happens.

Until we started our protests, people thought they had to follow rules no matter how weird the rules were. We reminded them that just because someone says something is the way it should be, it doesn't mean that's the way it should be.

In school, things settled down once lit circle ended. Ms. Sett packed the censored books up in their boxes and put them back in her closet. I don't know what she'll do with them; I don't know if she'll ever hand them out to other students. She seems not to have changed or opened her mind, and maybe that's just how some people are.

Mid-November rolled around and pizza delivery was allowed again. Also, the house paint ordinance was changed to include ten other colors.

"I just hope we can buy Cheetos here before I graduate high school," Denis says at recess a few days after the mid-November meeting.

Marci says, "I predict it will happen a lot faster than that."

Marci and I decided to be best friends and not be anything more serious because we're twelve. We both know we like each other. But it's better to hang out with Denis and be friends. The three of us did a poetry-pottery workshop with Sage Jones last weekend. My haiku saucer reads:

> important is truth
> even if it hurts sometimes
> it is still the truth

The week before Thanksgiving break, we even invent a new way to play BOT DUCK MAN with three players. The school is decorated with handprint turkeys and an occasional Native American and Pilgrim display.

Okay, look. I don't want to offend anyone, so I'm not even going to talk about Thanksgiving. I know it's Marci's favorite holiday because it's all about family and doesn't involve gifts. I used to really like it, too, because I love turkey, and Grandad and I always take a walk, even if it's freezing, and feed the ducks.

But the whole idea and the story they gave us for Thanksgiving is just not something I want to talk about ever again. And the fact that we still all gather on this day and eat and celebrate family while the families whose land we live on are not celebrating Thanksgiving because all we gave them was . . .

I said I wouldn't talk about it.

I won't talk about it.

And I want you to have a really great Thanksgiving.

But I also want you to think about the truth of the whole thing and at least try to figure out why some people don't really believe in celebrating Thanksgiving because it's not the real story.

Also, it's a billion-dollar business now, so the idea of

it being a sacred family holiday is sorta lost on me.

Crap. I said I wouldn't say anything.

Just—make your own mind up.

That's what happens next.

What happens next is people start making their own minds up about all kinds of things. Based on the truth.

When I sit and talk to Grandad at the end of the day, sitting in lotus position and rolling our beads in our hands, we daydream.

"I wish for a day when all people are truly treated like equals and have the same chances as everyone else," he says.

"I wish for a day when the truth isn't hidden in the long grass," I say.

Mom doesn't contact Dad anymore, but he's still in touch with Grandad, who updates him about me. For now, we're all taking a break from each other. He's seeing a therapist who is going to help him with being mad all the time and also with the stories he makes up.

I think of Jane Yolen and how she told me to find one thing I like about Dad. I'm still working on it.

What happens next, if we let it happen, is the truth sets us free.

Even if it makes us uncomfortable or sad.

It's still better to know the truth than it is to be lied to.

What happens next is the adults around here realize that there is no such thing as a perfect town, so they can stop feeling ashamed of the cool little town they already have.

What happens next is: I will go to middle school. Denis will be able to buy Cheetos on Main Street. Marci will be allowed to start an official feminism club. We will all listen to punk rock and dance accordingly. Three best friends take on the world and win.

Anything is possible now.

We just keep being ourselves.

That's what happens next.

Acknowledgments / Author's Note

Reader, I have to tell you—this novel was born from a true story.

Jane Yolen's *The Devil's Arithmetic* was censored in my local elementary school in the exact way as it's described here. After buying an uncensored copy at my local independent bookstore, I went to the principal to fix the problem, but I was shrugged off as if I was crazy to think that censorship is wrong.

Now, four years later, school districts all over the country are seeing a massive rise in book bans—where just a few citizens are removing many books from shelves in a call to "protect" you from the truth . . . when taking away stories of people different from you, or stories where you might be able to see yourself and your family, or, really, any stories, is the opposite of protection.

I want you to care about intellectual freedom— which is the right to read. I'm pretty sure if you got this far in the book, you do care, and you're probably sick of being treated like someone who knows less than you know. Good. Keep it up. My side of the deal is that I'll keep reminding adults that they need to listen to you more.

If your school is facing book challenges and bans, you can find information on how to fight them at: PEN America (https://pen.org/how-to-fight-book-bans-a-tip-sheet-for -students/) and the National Coalition Against Censorship (https://ncac.org/resource/book-censorship-toolkit). I could talk about this topic all day, and during Banned Books Week (yep—that's a real thing!), I do! But for now, I need to thank a few people.

Huge thanks to everyone at Scholastic, but an extra-big fist bump to David Levithan, my editor and my friend. More huge thanks to Michael Bourret, the best agent in the galaxy.

Enormous thanks to Jane Yolen for writing amazing books and for letting me write about her. Jane, thank you for what you do for young people. My admiration is endless.

Huge props to my kid, who is not Mac Delaney, but who is as fearless, and to my parents, who taught me to seek truth, no matter what, which made me into a writer.

Teachers, Librarians, Booksellers: Thank you for everything. <3

About the Author

Amy Sarig King is the author of the critically acclaimed novels *The Year We Fell From Space* and *Me and Marvin Gardens*. She has also published many award-winning young adult novels under the name A. S. King including *Dig*, the 2020 Michael L. Printz Award winner; *Please Ignore Vera Dietz*, a Michael L. Printz Honor book; and *Ask the Passengers*, which won the Los Angeles Times Book Prize. She is the recipient of the 2022 Margaret A. Edwards Award for a lasting contribution to young adult literature, and lives in Pennsylvania with her epic kid. Visit her website at as-king.com.